For Molly Lajtha

*(plus a big thank you to
Emma Chadwick-Booth)*

One

I thought it was going to be the best Christmas ever. I woke up very very early and sat up as slowly as I could, trying not to shake the bed. I didn't want to wake Vita or Maxie. I wanted to have this moment all to myself.

I wriggled down to the end of the bed, carefully edging round Vita. She always curled up like a little monkey, knees right under her pointed chin, so the hump that was her stopped halfway down the duvet. It was so dark I couldn't see at all, but I could feel.

My hand stroked three little woolly socks stretched to bursting point. They were tiny stripy socks, too small even for Vita. The joke was to see how many weeny presents could be stuffed inside.

Vita and Maxie appreciated Santa's sense of humour and left him a minute mince pie on a doll's tea-set plate and a thimbleful of wine, and wrote him teeny thank-you letters on pieces of paper no bigger than a postage stamp. Well, Vita couldn't fit her shaky pencil printing on such a tiny scrap but she wrote *'Dear Santa I love you and pleese leeve me*

3

lots and lots of little pressents from your speshal frend Vita' on a big piece of paper and then folded it up again and again. Maxie simply wrote a letter 'M' and a lot of wonky kisses.

I wrote a letter too, even though I was only pretending for Vita and Maxie's sake. I knew who filled the Christmas socks. I thought he was much more magical than any bearded old gent in a red gown.

I felt past the socks to the space underneath. My hand brushed three parcels wrapped in crackly paper and tied with silk ribbon. I felt their shapes, wondering which one was for me. There was a very small square hard parcel, a flat oblong package and a large unwieldy squashy one, very wide at one end. I hung further out of bed, trying to work out the peculiar shape. I wriggled a little too far and went scooting right over the end, landing on my head.

Maxie woke up and started shrieking.

'Ssh! Shut up, Maxie! It's OK, don't cry,' I said, crawling past the presents to Maxie's little mattress.

He doesn't want to sleep in a proper bed. He likes to set up a camp with lots of blankets and cushions and all his cuddly toys. Sometimes it's hard to spot Maxie himself under all his droopy old teddies.

I wrestled my way through a lot of fur and found Maxie, quivering in his going-to-bed jersey and underpants. That's another weird thing about Maxie, he hates pyjamas. There are a *lot* of weird things about my little brother.

I crawled onto his mattress and cuddled him close. 'It's me, silly.'

'I thought you were a Wild Thing coming to get

me,' Maxie sobbed.

Where the Wild Things Are was Dad's favourite book. The little boy in it is called Max, and he tames all these Wild Thing monsters. That's where our Maxie got his name. Reading the book to him was a *big* mistake. Our Maxie couldn't ever tame Wild Thing scary monsters. He wouldn't be up to taming wild fluffy baby bunnies.

'The Wild Things are all shut up in their book, Maxie,' I whispered. 'Stop crying, you'll make my nightie all wet. Cheer up, it's Christmas!'

'Is Father Christmas here?' Vita shouted, jumping out from under the duvet.

'Ssh! It's only six o'clock. But he's been, he's left us presents.'

'Has he left any presents for me?' said Maxie.

'No, none whatsoever,' said Vita, jumping down the bed and pouncing on the presents. 'Yay! *For dear Vita, love from Santa*. And here we are again— *To darling Vita, even more love from Santa*. And there's this one too, *To my special sweetheart Vita, lots and lots and lots of love from Santa*. Nothing for you two at all.'

Maxie started sobbing again.

'She's just teasing, Maxie. Don't let her wind you up. Shut *up*, Vita. Be nice, it's Christmas. Leave the presents *alone*. We open them in Mum and Dad's bed, you know we do.'

'Let's go to their room now!' said Vita, scrabbling at the bottom of the bed, scooping up all three parcels and clutching them to her chest.

'No, no, it's not time yet. Mum will be cross,' I said, unpeeling Maxie and jumping up to restrain Vita.

'My daddy won't be cross with me,' said Vita.

5

I always hated it when she said *my* daddy. It was a mean Vita trick to remind me that he wasn't really *my* dad.

He always said he loved me just as much as Vita and Maxie. I hoped hoped hoped it was true, because I loved him more than anyone else in the whole world, even a tiny bit more than Mum. More than Vita and Maxie. Much more than Gran.

'We'd better wait until seven, Vita,' I said.

'No!'

'Half past six then. Mum and Dad were out till late last night, they'll be tired.'

'They won't be tired, it's Christmas! Stop being so boring, Em. You just want to boss me about all the time.'

It's almost impossible to boss Vita even though she's years younger than me and literally half my size. She's the one who's done the bossing, ever since she could sit up in her buggy and shriek. It is a royal pain having a little sister like Vita. You have to learn to be dead crafty if you want to manage her.

'If you come and cuddle back into bed I'll tell you another Princess Vita story,' I said. 'A special *Christmas* Princess Vita story where she gets to fly to Santa's workshop and has the pick of all his presents. And she meets Mrs Christmas and all the little children Christmases—Clara Christmas, Caroline Christmas and little Charlie Christmas.'

'Can Prince Maxie play with Charlie Christmas?' said Maxie.

'No, he can't. This is *my* Princess Vita story,' said Vita.

I had her hooked. She got back into bed. Maxie grabbed an armful of teddies and climbed into our

6

bed too. I lay between them, making up the story. Princess Vita stories were very *boring* because they always had to be about sweetly pretty show-off Princess Vita. Everyone adored her and wanted to be her friend and gave her elaborate presents. I had to go into extreme detail describing each designer princess gown with matching wings, her jewelled ten-league trainers, and the golden crown the exact shade of Princess Vita's long long curls.

Our Vita wriggled and squirmed excitedly, and when I started describing the golden crown (and the pink diamond tiara and the ruby slides and the amethyst hair bobbles) she tossed her head around as if she was adorning her own long long curls. She hasn't really got any. Vita has very thin, fine, straight baby hair like beige cotton. She's been growing it for several years but it still hasn't reached her shoulders.

My hair is straw rather than mouse, and thick and strong. When I undo my plaits it very nearly reaches my waist (if I tilt my head right back).

'*Please* put Prince Maxie into the story,' Maxie begged, nuzzling his head against my neck. His hair is the same length as Vita's, coal-black with a long fringe. If he's wriggled around a lot in the night it sticks straight out like a chimney brush.

'Princess Vita has a brother called Prince Maxie, the boldest biggest boy in the whole kingdom,' I said.

Maxie sucked in his breath with pleasure.

'As if!' said Vita. 'Bother Prince Maxie. Tell about Princess Vita's trip to see Santa.'

I ended up telling *two* stories, swerving from one to the other, five minutes of Princess Vita, a quick diversion to see Prince Maxie defeating the seven-

7

headed dragon spouting scarlet flames, and then back to Princess Vita's sortie in Santa's sleigh.

'There aren't *really* seven-headed dragons, are there?' said Maxie.

'No, you've killed the very last one,' I said.

'How do you know there aren't any more hiding in their caves?' Maxie asked.

'Oh yes, there are lots and lots, all huddled down in the dark so you can't see them, but they come creeping out at night all ready to *get* you,' Vita said gleefully.

'Will you stop being so mean to him, you bad girl!' I said. 'I'll torture you!' I got hold of her stick wrist and gave her a tiny Chinese burn.

'Didn't hurt,' Vita laughed. 'No one can hurt me. I'm Princess Vita. If any monsters come bothering me I'll give them one kick with my ten league trainers and they'll beg for mercy.'

'OK, let's get *you* begging for mercy. I'm going to tickle you,' I said, scrabbling under her chin, in her armpit, on her tummy.

Vita giggled and kicked and squirmed, trying to burrow under the duvet away from me.

'Come on, Maxie, let's get her,' I said.

'Tickle tickle tickle,' said Maxie, his hands shaped into little claws. He stabbed at Vita ineffectively. She was in such a giggly heap she squealed anyway.

'I'm tickling Vita!' Maxie said proudly.

'Yeah, look, she's cowering away from you,' I said. 'But there's no escape, little Vita, the tickle torturers are relentless.'

I reached right under the duvet and found her feet. I held one captive with one hand and tickled the other.

'No, no, stop it, you beast!' Vita screamed, threshing and kicking.

'Hey, hey, who's being murdered?' Dad came into the room, hands on his hips, just wearing his jeans.

'*Dad!*' We all three yelled his name and jumped at him for a big hug. 'Merry Christmas, Dad!'

'Santa's been, Dad, look!'

'He left lots of presents—all for *me*!' said Vita.

'You wish, little Vita,' said Dad. He caught her up and whirled her round and round.

'Me too, me too,' Maxie begged.

'No, little Maxie, we're going to toss you like a pancake,' said Dad, picking Maxie up and hurling him high in the air. Maxie shrieked in terror, but bore it because he didn't want to be left out.

I didn't want to be left out either but I knew there was no way Dad could whirl or toss me. I sat back on the bed feeling larger and lumpier than ever. Dad pretended to take a bite out of Maxie pancake and then set him free. Dad smiled at me. He bowed formally.

'Would you care to dance, Princess Glittering Green Emerald?'

I jumped up and Dad started doing this crazy jive with me, singing a rock 'n' roll version of 'Rudolph the Red-Nosed Reindeer'. Vita and Maxie started jumping around too, Vita light as a feather, Maxie thumping.

'Hey, hey, calm down now, kids, we'll wake Mum.'

'We *want* to wake Mum,' said Vita. 'We want our presents!'

'OK, let's go and wish her happy Christmas,' said Dad. 'Bring the presents into our room.'

9

'They aren't really all for Vita, are they, Dad?' said Maxie.

'There's one each for all of you,' said Dad. '*That* one is for my number one son.'

'I'm your number one daughter, aren't I, Dad?' said Vita, elbowing me out of the way.

'You're my special *little* daughter,' said Dad.

I waited. I didn't want to be his *big* daughter.

'You're my special grown-up daughter, Emerald,' said Dad.

My name isn't *really* Emerald, it's plain Emily. All the rest of the family called me Em. I *loved* it when Dad called me Emerald.

'Shall I go and make you and Mum a cup of tea?' I offered.

I loved being treated like a grown-up too. Vita and Maxie weren't allowed anywhere near the cooker and couldn't so much as switch on the kettle.

'That would be great, darling, but if you start faffing around in the kitchen your gran will wake up.'

'Ah. Right.' We certainly didn't want Gran climbing into Mum and Dad's bed with us.

'Come on then, kids. Let's get the Christmas show on the road,' said Dad. He yawned and ran his fingers through his long hair. My dad's got the most beautiful long hair in the whole world. It's thick and dark and glossy black, like Maxie's, but Dad's grown his way past his shoulders. He wears it in one tight fat plait during the day to keep it neat, and then it's all lovely and loose at night. It looks so strange and special, so perfect for Dad. He gets fed up with it sometimes, saying he looks like some silly old hippy, and he's always threatening to get it cut.

That's how Dad met Mum. He went into her hairdressing salon at the top of the Pink Palace on the spur of the moment and asked her to chop it all off. She took one look at him and said no way. She said she didn't usually go for guys with long hair but said it really suited Dad and it would be a shame to spoil such a distinctive look. That's what she said. I knew this story off by heart. Dad liked her paying him compliments so he asked her if she'd come for a drink with him when she finished work. They ended up spending the whole evening together and falling madly in love. They've been together ever since. Just like a fairy story. They don't live in an enchanted castle because Mum doesn't earn that much money as a hairdresser and Dad earns less as an actor, though he has his fairy stall at the Pink Palace now. He works very hard, no matter what Gran says.

We tiptoed along the landing so as not to wake her. She has the biggest bedroom at the front. I suppose that's only fair as it's her house, but it means Mum and Dad are squashed up in the little bedroom, and Vita, Maxie and me are positively crammed into our room. Gran suggested one of us might like to go and sleep in her room with her but we thought that was a terrible idea.

Gran snores for a start. We could hear her snoring on Christmas morning even though her bedroom door was shut. Dad gave a very tiny piggy snore, imitating her, and we all got the giggles. We had to hold our hands over our mouths to muffle them (not easy clutching Christmas stockings and slippery parcels!). We exploded into Mum and Dad's bedroom, dropping everything, jumping on

11

the bed, snorting with laughter.

Mum sat up, startled, her hair hanging in her eyes. 'What . . . ?' she mumbled.

'Merry Christmas, Mum!'

'Happy Christmas, babe,' said Dad, kissing her.

'Oh darling, happy happy Christmas,' said Mum, flinging her arms round him and running her fingers through his hair.

'Give *me* a Christmas kiss, Mum!' Vita demanded, pulling at her bare shoulder.

'Me too,' said Maxie.

'Me too, me too, me too!' I said, making a joke of it, sending them up.

'Happy Christmas, kids. Big big kisses for all of you in just a minute,' said Mum, wrapping her dressing gown round her and climbing out of bed.

'Hey, where are you going?' said Dad, climbing back in. 'Come back!'

'Got to take a little trip to the bathroom, darling,' said Mum.

We couldn't be mean enough to start opening our stockings without her. She kept us waiting a little while. She came back smelling of toothpaste and her special rosy soap, her face powdered, her hair teased and sprayed into her usual blonde bob.

'Come on, babe, come and cuddle up,' said Dad, hitching Vita and Maxie along to make room for her.

He ruffled Mum's hair like she was a little kid too. Mum didn't moan, even though she'd just made it perfect. She waited until Dad was helping Maxie with his stocking and then she quickly patted her hair back into shape, smoothing down her fringe and tweaking the ends. She wasn't being vain. She was just trying extra hard to look nice for

Dad.

We had this tradition of opening presents in turn, starting with the youngest, but this wasn't such a good idea with Maxie. He was so slow, delicately picking out the first tiny parcel from his stocking, prodding it warily and then cautiously shaking it, as if he thought it might be a miniature bomb. When he decided it was safe to open he spent ages nudging the edge of the sellotape with his thumbnail.

'Hurry *up*, Maxie,' Vita said impatiently. 'Just pull the paper.'

'I don't want to rip it, it looks so pretty. I want to wrap all my presents up again after I've seen what they are,' said Maxie.

'Here, son, let me help,' said Dad, and within a minute or two he'd shelled all Maxie's stocking presents out of their shiny paper.

Maxie cupped his hands to hold them all at once: his magic pencil that could draw red and green and blue and yellow all in one go; a silver spiral notebook; a weeny yellow plastic duck no bigger than his thumb; a tiny toy tractor; a mini box of Smarties; a little watch on a plastic strap; a green glass marble; and a pair of his very own nail clippers (Maxie always wants to borrow Dad's).

'How does Santa know exactly what I like?' said Maxie.

'How indeed?' said Dad solemnly.

'Will you help me wrap them all up now, Dad?'

'Yeah, of course I will.'

'I'm unwrapping mine!' said Vita, spilling her goodies all over the duvet, ripping each one open with her scrabbly little fingers. She found a tiny pink lady ornament in a ballet frock; sparkly

13

butterfly hairslides; a set of kitten and puppy stickers; a miniature red box of raisins; a weeny purple brush and comb set; a little book about a rabbit with print so tiny you could hardly read it; a bead necklace spelling I LOVE VITA; and her very own real lipstick.

'I hope Santa's given you a very pale pink lipstick,' said Mum. 'Go on then, Em, open your stocking.'

I was getting too big to believe in Santa but he still wanted to please me. I found a little orange journal with its own key; a tiny red heart soap; a purple gel pen; cherry bobbles for my hair; a tiny tin of violet sweets; a Miffy eraser; a Jenna Williams bookmark; and a small pot of silver glitter nail varnish.

'I love that colour,' said Mum. 'Santa's got good taste, Em. I wish he'd leave me a stocking.'

'You've got *our* presents, Mum,' I said.

They weren't really special enough. We always made our presents for Mum and Dad, and so they looked like rubbish. Maxie did a drawing of Mum and Dad and Vita and me, but we weren't exactly recognizable. We looked like five potatoes on toothpicks.

Vita did a family portrait too. She drew herself very big, her head touching one end of the paper and her feet the other. She embellished herself with very long thick hair and silver shoes with enormously high heels. She drew Dad one side of her, Mum the other, using up so much space she had to squash Maxie and me high up in either corner, just our heads and shoulders, looking down like gargoyles.

I felt I was too old for drawing silly pictures. I

wanted to make them proper presents. Gran had recently taught me to knit, so at the beginning of December I'd started to knit a woollen patchwork quilt for Mum and Dad's bed. I knitted and knitted and knitted—in the playground, watching television, on the loo—but by Christmas Eve I had only managed eleven squares, not even enough for a newborn baby's quilt.

I sewed the prettiest pink square into a weird pouch done up with a pearly button. It was too holey for a purse but I thought Mum could maybe keep her comb inside. I sewed the other ten squares into one long scarf for Dad. It wasn't exactly the right shape and it rolled over at the edges but I hoped he might still like it.

'I absolutely love it, Em,' he said, wrapping it round his neck. 'I've wanted a long stripy scarf ever since I watched *Dr Who* when I was a little kid. Thank you, darling.' He stroked the uneven rows. 'It's so cosy! I'll be as warm as toast all winter.'

I felt my cheeks glowing. I knew he probably hated it and didn't want to be seen dead wearing it, but he made me believe he truly loved it at the same time.

Mum gave him a v-necked soft black sweater and he put it on at once, but he kept my scarf round his neck.

'What about *my* present?' Mum asked, as eagerly as Vita.

'What present?' said Dad, teasing her. Then he reached underneath the bed and handed her an oblong package. She felt the parcel and then tore off the wrapping. A pair of silver shoes tumbled out, strappy sandals with the highest heels ever.

'Oh my God!' Mum shrieked. 'They're so

15

beautiful. Oh darling, how wicked, how glamorous, how incredible!' She started kissing Dad rapturously.

'Hey, hey, they're just *shoes*,' he said. 'Come on then, kids, open your big presents.'

He helped Maxie unwrap an enormous set of expensive Caran d'Ache colouring pens and a big white pad of special artist's paper.

'But he's just a little kid, Frankie. He'll press too hard and ruin the tips,' Mum said.

'No *I won't*, Mum!' said Maxie.

'*He will*,' I mouthed at Mum. Maxie had already totally ruined the red and the sky-blue in *my* set of felt pens. I couldn't help feeling envious of Maxie's beautiful set, so superior to my own.

'My turn, my turn, my turn!' Vita shouted, tearing at her huge parcel. One weird long brown twisty thing poked through the paper as she scrabbled at it, then another.

'What *is* it?' Vita shrieked.

Then she discovered a big pink nose.

'Is it a clown?' Maxie asked fearfully.

Dad had taken us to the circus in the summer and Maxie had spent most of the evening under his seat, terrified of the clowns.

'Try pressing that nose,' said Dad.

Vita poked at it, and it played a pretty tinkly tune.

'That's "The Sugar Plum Fairy" from some ballet. We did it in music,' I said.

Vita tore the last of the paper away to reveal the huge sweet head of a furry reindeer, with two twisty plush antlers sticking out at angles. She had big brown glass eyes, fantastic long eyelashes, and a smiley red-lined mouth with a soft pink tongue. She

16

was wearing a pink ballet dress with a satin bodice and net skirt.

'I love her, I love her!' Vita declared, hugging her passionately to her chest.

The reindeer had long floppy furry legs with pink satin ballet slippers, but she couldn't stand on them. I lifted the net skirt and saw a big hole.

'Don't look up her bottom!' Vita snapped.

'Um, Em's being rude,' said Maxie.

'No, I'm not! I've just realized, she's a glove puppet!'

'You got it, Emerald,' said Dad. 'Here, Vita, let's get to know her. We'll see if she'll introduce herself.'

He pressed her pink nose again to stop the ballet music and stuck his hand up inside her.

'Hello, Princess Vita,' he made the reindeer say, in a funny fruity female voice. 'I'm Dancer. I was one of Santa's very own reindeers. Maybe you've heard of my fellow sleigh artistes, Dasher and Prancer and Vixen? Then there's the so-called superstar, Rudolph, the one with the constant cold. *Such* a show-off, especially since he got his own song. Of course *I* was always the leading runner, until I realized that all that sleigh-pulling wasn't such a good idea. I have very sensitive hooves. Santa was devastated when I gave in my notice but we artistes have to consider our talent. I am now Princess Vita's dancing companion and trusty steed.'

Dad made Dancer bow low and then twirl on her floppety legs. Vita clapped her hands, bright red with excitement.

I felt envious again. Why couldn't *I* have had a puppet? Then Dad and I could have had endless

17

games together. Vita and Maxie had such special big presents this year. Why did mine have to be so tiny? It was just like one extra stocking present.

'Aren't you going to open your present, Emerald?' said Dad. He slipped Dancer over Vita's hand, showing her how to work her. Vita waved her wildly round and round. Maxie laughed and tried to catch Dancer. One of her antlers accidently poked him in the eye.

'Hey, hey, watch out! Oh Maxie, for heaven's sake, it didn't really hurt,' said Mum, grabbing Vita's arm and pulling Maxie close for a cuddle. 'Yes, Em, open your present. Whatever can it be?'

I undid the wrapping paper, feeling foolish with them all watching me. I got my mouth all puckered up, waiting to say *Thank you* and give grateful kisses. Then I opened a little black box and stared at what was inside. I was stunned. I couldn't say anything at all.

'What is it, Em?'

'Show us!'

'Don't you like it?'

It was a little gold ring set with a deep green glowing jewel.

'I *love* it,' I whispered. 'It's an emerald!'

'Not a real emerald, darling,' said Mum.

'Yes it is,' said Dad. 'I'm not fobbing off my daughter with anything less!'

My *daughter*! I loved that almost as much as my beautiful ring.

'Don't be silly, Frankie,' Mum said. '*Real* emeralds cost hundreds and hundreds of pounds!'

'No they don't. Not if you go to antique fairs and do someone a favour and find a little emerald for a special small girl,' said Dad.

18

He unhooked the ring from its little velvet cushion and put it on the ring finger of my right hand.

'It fits perfectly!' I said.

'Well, I had it made specially for you, Princess Emerald,' said Dad.

'But however much have you spent on all of us?' Mum said, shaking her head as if she'd been swimming underwater.

'Never you mind,' said Dad. 'I wanted this to be a special Christmas, one the kids will remember for ever.'

'But we owe so much already—'

'Leave it, Julie,' Dad said sharply.

So Mum left it. We had a big Christmas cuddle, the five of us—six, counting Dancer—and then we heard Gran going downstairs to put the kettle on.

Vita insisted on having Dancer on her lap at breakfast time. Maxie held onto his felt tips too, balancing them across his bony knees. I stuck my hand out after every mouthful, admiring my ring.

'Haven't we got the loveliest dad ever?' said Vita.

Gran sniffed. 'What have you done now, Frankie, robbed a bank?' she said.

Dad laughed and put his arm round her. 'Now, Ellen, no po-faces, it's Christmas. Come on, you old bat, you know you love me really.' He gave her a kiss. She pushed him away, shaking her head, but she couldn't help smiling. She actually burst out laughing when she opened *her* present from Dad. It was a pair of tight designer jeans.

'For God's sake, Frankie, I'm a grandma!'

'And you've got almost as lovely a figure as your daughter, so flaunt it, eh? You'll look great in the jeans, much better than those baggy old trousers. Try them on!'

'Don't think you can get round *me*,' said Gran—but she changed into her new jeans after breakfast.

Dad was right. Gran had a really good figure, though we'd never noticed it before. From the waist down she didn't look a bit like our gran. Dad gave her a wolf whistle and she told him not to be so daft—but she blushed.

'I'm not going to wear them *out* of course,' she said. 'Still, they're fine for the house.'

*   *   *

She had to go and change out of them again after Christmas dinner. We normally all eat separately. Vita and Maxie and I have our tea after school. Mum just has snacks while she's waiting to have a meal later with Dad. Gran heats up her own Lean Cuisines and eats them off a tray when *EastEnders* and *Coronation Street* are on television. But Christmas is different. We all eat together with a proper tablecloth and Gran's best white-and-gold china from the cabinet where she keeps her pink crinoline lady and the balloon-seller and the little mermaid with a green scaly tail and the little girl and boy in white china nightgowns.

We had crackers so we all wore paper hats and shouted out silly mottoes. Vita snorted with laughter while she was drinking her Ribena 'wine' and it went right up her nose and then spattered the white embroidered cloth. Gran would have gone mad if Maxie or I had done it, but she just shook her head fondly at Vita and told her to calm down.

20

Vita made a fuss about her Christmas dinner too. She wouldn't eat a single sprout or parsnip and only one forkful of turkey. She just wanted a plate of roast potatoes.

'Well, why shouldn't the kid have exactly what she fancies on Christmas Day?' said Dad, scraping everything off her plate and then piling it high with potatoes.

Maxie started noisily demanding a plate of roast potatoes too. Mum and Gran sighed at Dad for starting something.

'Still, at least our Em's eating her plateful,' said Mum.

'Em always eats everything. It's a wonder she doesn't gollop the plate down too,' said Gran.

She'd started to nag me about calories and carbohydrates and all that stuff, though Mum always got mad at her and said she'd turn me anorexic.

'As if!' said Gran unkindly.

I took no notice and munched my way through my turkey and chipolata sausages and roast potatoes and mashed potatoes and parsnips and every single sprout and then I had a slice of Christmas pudding with green jelly and red jelly and cream and then a mince pie and then a satsuma and *then* three chocolates out of the Christmas tin of Quality Street.

Gran slapped my hand away when I reached in the tin for a fourth chocolate. 'For God's sake, Em, you'll burst,' she said. 'Your stomach must be made of elastic. You'll have to learn to stop shovelling your food up like that. I don't know how you *can*. I'm totally stuffed. I'm going to have to take my posh jeans off and have a little lie down.'

21

'Quit nagging Princess Emerald. It's great that she's got a healthy appetite,' said Dad. 'Right, ladies, us chaps will do the washing-up. You can all take a little nap. We'll do the donkey work in the kitchen, won't we, Maxie?'

Maxie took Dad seriously and started gathering Gran's best china with a bang and a clatter.

'Hey, hey, careful, you'll chip those plates!' said Gran.

'Yeah, Gran's got a point, little guy,' said Dad. 'Tell you what, you start drawing me a lovely picture with your new felt pens. Then I can get on with the washing-up in peace.'

Maxie lay on the floor, carefully colouring, his eyes screwed up and his tongue sticking out because he was concentrating so fiercely. He was *much* more careful with the points of his own felt tips than he was with mine.

Vita annoyed him for a while, running her fingers over the felt pens in the tin, playing them as if they were an instrument, but her roast potatoes took a toll on her. She lay back on the sofa, Dancer on her arm so she could use her velvety head like a cuddle blanket. Mum curled up in a corner of the sofa. She said she wanted to watch the Queen on television but her eyes started drooping and she was asleep in seconds.

I sat back, my hand stretched out in front of me, so I could admire my real emerald from every angle. I still couldn't believe how wonderful it was. Dad said he'd got it at a bargain price but I knew it still must have cost heaps. More than Mum's silver sandals or Gran's jeans or Vita's reindeer or Maxie's crayons.

It must mean that Dad loved me just as much as

22

Vita and Maxie even though I wasn't really his daughter. I knew I loved him more than anyone. Far far far far far far far more than my own dad.

I hadn't seen him for years now. I didn't want to. We didn't want to have any more to do with him, Mum and me.

I decided to go and help Dad with the washing-up, even though he'd told us all he wanted the kitchen to himself. I crept across the living room into the hall. I waved at my ring in the mirror above the telephone table. It winked its brilliant green light back at me.

The kitchen door was shut. I could hear Dad muttering inside. I grinned. Was he singing to himself as he did the dishes? I opened the door slowly and carefully, not making a sound. Dad had his back to me.

'Oh darling, darling, darling,' he said.

I thought he was talking to me. Then I saw the hunch of his shoulders, his hand up against his ear. He was talking on his mobile.

'Yeah, yeah! Oh Sarah, I'm missing you so much too,' he said. 'Still, I can't get out of Christmas, it means so much to Julie and the kids. I'm trying to make it happy for them, though dear God it's such an effort now. Still, I'm planning on telling them soon. I can't stay much longer. I'm going crazy. I want to be with you so badly, babe. I'm leaving them, I swear I am.'

'Don't leave us, Dad!'

He whipped round. I waited for him to tell me I'd got it all wrong. He wasn't really talking to some girlfriend. He was acting a part, playing some stupid joke. Dad could always talk his way out of anything. I wanted him to tell me any old story,

23

even if I knew he was lying.

He didn't say anything. He just stood staring at me, biting his lip foolishly the way Maxie does when he's been caught out. The mobile phone buzzed as someone spoke to him.

'Call you back,' Dad said and he switched the phone off. He held it warily, as if it was a hand grenade.

We stared at each other, standing freeze-framed. I wished I could rewind a minute so I could be back in the hall, happily waving my emerald ring around.

'You're not really leaving us, are you, Dad?' I whispered.

'I'm sorry, Em,' he said softly.

The room started spinning. I staggered to the sink and threw up all over the china in the washing-up bowl.

Two

'It's all right, Em, it's all right,' Dad said, holding me.

We both knew it could never be all right again. I retched and sobbed, unable to reply.

Gran came bursting into the kitchen, disturbed from her nap.

'What's going on? Oh, for God's sake, you've been sick all over my best china!'

'Who's been sick?' said Mum, coming in too. Vita and Maxie followed her.

'Em's been sick,' said Gran. 'I *told* you not to make a pig of yourself, Emily.'

'Yuck!' said Vita.

'It smells!' said Maxie.

'You two, out of here,' said Mum. 'Go into the living room with your gran. I'll clear it all up.'

'Maybe you'll listen to me when I tell you that child should stop stuffing herself. God, what a mess! It's even splashed on the curtains!' Gran was nearly in tears herself.

'I'll wash everything. Just leave us alone, please,' said Dad.

He said it very quietly, but Gran stopped fussing and dragged Vita and Maxie out of the kitchen.

'Oh, Em,' said Mum, dabbing at me with a tea towel. 'We'd better pull these things off and stick you straight in the bath. Couldn't you have run to the toilet if you were going to be so sick?'

'It wasn't her fault,' said Dad. He was so grey-white he looked like he might be sick himself.

'What do you mean? What's going on?' said Mum, trying to hitch my sweater over my head.

'Don't tell her, Dad!' I said through layers of soggy wool.

If he kept quiet then maybe it wouldn't be real.

'I was planning on telling you anyway, but I was leaving it till after Christmas. I'm so sorry. I just hate myself for doing this to you. I didn't mean it to happen.'

'What the hell are you talking about?' said Mum, letting go off me.

Dad took a deep breath. 'I've met someone else, Julie.'

Mum scarcely blinked. 'Yes. Well. That's nothing new,' she said.

'But this time, well, I love her. I'm sorry, I don't want to hurt you, but this is it, the real thing. It's never been this way before.'

'You don't want to hurt me and yet you're telling me you love someone else?' said Mum, her face crumpling.

'Oh, Mum, don't cry,' I begged. I wanted to put my arms round her but I was so wet and disgusting I couldn't touch her.

'Go and get in the bath, Em,' Dad said. 'Your mum and I need to talk.'

'*I* need to talk too,' I said. 'You love *us*, Dad—

28

Mum and me and Vita and Maxie.'

'Of course I love you, darling. I shall come and visit you lots, but I can't help it. I have to go.'

'You can't do this to me! You can't, you can't!' Mum started sobbing, swaying on her silver sandals.

Dad tried to put his arm round her but she started hitting him.

'Don't, Mum, don't, Dad!' I shouted.

I couldn't believe this was happening. I kept shutting my eyes and opening them, hoping that I was dreaming. If only I could open my eyes determinedly enough I'd get back to our magical Christmas Day.

Gran came back in the kitchen and she started shouting too. Then she was propelling me out of the room, dragging me upstairs to the bathroom, stripping the rest of my clothes off and dunking me in the bath like a baby. She soaped me so hard it felt like she was slapping me.

Vita and Maxie kept tapping on the bathroom door, crying to be let in.

'Oh, for God's sake,' said Gran, shampooing my hair because some of it had dangled in the sick. Her nails dug right into my scalp.

I didn't dare tell her she was hurting me. She seemed so terrifyingly cross with me, as if it was all my fault.

Maybe it was *my fault*.

Vita and Maxie seemed ready to blame me. They came hurtling into the bathroom.

'Mum's mad at Dad because you were sick everywhere, Em,' said Vita.

'She's shouting and shouting. She even shouted at me though *I* wasn't sick,' Maxie wept.

They didn't seem to understand what was really going on. They were too little. I wanted to be too little too. Gran was bathing me like a baby. I wanted to *be* a baby. I wanted her to wrap me in the towel and pick me up and hug me close. She must have made a proper fuss of me when I was a baby—all grans did.

'There, Em, get out the bath. Don't just stand there looking gormless,' Gran snapped. 'Get yourself dry and then get some clean clothes on.'

She yanked at me so that I nearly overbalanced. My emerald gleamed as I waved my arms in the air.

'Oh, Gran, my ring! I've got it all wet and soapy! Oh no, what if I've spoiled it!' I gasped.

'Yes, well, it was ridiculous giving a child your age an emerald ring,' said Gran. 'Typical badword Frankie!'

It was *such* a bad word that we all stared at her. How dare she call my dad horrible names! I looked at her pale veiny legs showing through her dressing gown.

'It was ridiculous giving an old lady your age a pair of jeans,' I said.

Vita and Maxie gasped. I backed away from her rapidly because she looked like she was going to slap me. But she just sighed and shook her head at me, as if she'd simply caught me scratching or picking my nose. I realized she was too concerned with what was happening down in the kitchen to care about me cheeking her.

Mum was still screaming and sobbing, on and on and on.

When I was dry and dressed and in clean clothes Gran made Vita and Maxie and me stay shut up in the living room. She put the television volume up until it buzzed whenever anyone talked but we could still hear Mum in the kitchen. I kept switching channels until Gran snatched the remote out of my hand.

'Let's watch a video. Let's watch *Thomas*. Please, please, *Thomas*!' Maxie begged.

He hadn't watched *Thomas the Tank Engine* for months and months. He still knew it by heart. We *all* knew it by heart but we tried to watch it, even Gran. Mum was still shouting. Dad was shouting back now. Vita put her thumb in her mouth and rubbed her nose on Dancer's fur. Maxie kept his eyes on *Thomas* but under his breath he muttered, 'Bad Mummy, bad Daddy.'

I wished I had a remote for Mum and Dad so I could press their mute button. I kept telling myself that it would somehow be all right. They'd stop shouting and suddenly sigh and fall into each other's arms. They'd done this enough times in the past so they could do it again. Dad would say he'd been mad to think of leaving us. He'd swear he'd never see this Sarah again. He'd stay with Mum and Vita and Maxie and me and we'd all live happily ever after. I told myself this fairy story over and over, clenching my fists, my emerald ring digging into my skin.

'For pity's sake, look at you kids! It's Christmas!' said Gran.

She wrapped her dressing gown right round her and marched off to the kitchen, her bedroom slippers thwacking the floor at each step.

'She's gone to tell them off,' said Maxie.

It seemed to work. The shouting stopped. There was a lot of muttering. Then Gran came back into the living room. Dad came with her. His eyes were

31

red as if he'd been crying too, but he was smiling determinedly. He looked like his upturned lips had been stuck on his face by mistake.

'Right, my little lovelies, what do we all want to play, eh?'

'We could play Snap,' Maxie suggested.

He was useless at Snap, so slow at recognizing two identical cards that he simply screamed '*Snap!*' at the top of his voice all the time. Your ears ached when you played Snap with Maxie.

'Snap's stupid, and Maxie can't play it properly,' said Vita. 'Let's play Happy Families.'

Dad winced. Vita wasn't deliberately getting at him. She liked Happy Families because she loved the pictures of the rabbit and the squirrel and the mouse families.

'Let's play a Christmas game,' said Dad. He looked round for Dancer and put his hand up inside her.

'We'll all dance,' said Dancer. 'Let's play Musical Bumps.'

Dad shuffled through the CDs until he found an old *Children's Favourites* with silly songs about pink toothbrushes and mice with clogs and runaway trains.

'*Not* the red-nosed reindeer song!' Dancer said, jiggling about on the end of Dad's arm. 'OK, let's get jumping! Watch me pirouette, girls and boys!'

Dad played the music really loudly. Maxie and Vita started leaping around the living room. I started jumping too. Gran sighed.

'For heaven's sake, Em, do you have to thump like that? You're rattling all my china figurines in the cabinet.'

I stopped so abruptly I twisted my ankles.

32

'No, no, come on, Princess Emerald, you're light as a fairy,' Dad said. 'Let me sweep you up in my arms and we'll do a merry Christmas jig.'

'Yes, merry Christmas to you too, you dirty heart-breaking swine,' said Gran, and she ran out of the room.

Vita and Maxie stood still too.

'No, no, the music's not stopped yet. Don't you children know how to play Musical Bumps?' said Dancer.

So we jumped and we bumped regardless of Gran's china. Then Dancer taught us how to play all these old-fashioned party games like Squeak Piggy Squeak and Blind Man's Buff. Dad used my woollen scarf as a blindfold. Dancer admired the scarf and said she wished she'd had something similar for those cold nights pulling Santa's sleigh.

'A chic knitted scarf with matching antler-warmers—and woolly patchwork pants would be a great idea too!' she said.

We all collapsed in a heap on the carpet and Dad gave Vita and Maxie a cuddle. I wondered if I was too big for a little kid's cuddle but Dad reached out and pulled me in.

'Dad, you're not *really* going to go, are you?' I whispered right in his ear.

'Ssh, Princess Emerald! We won't discuss state secrets in front of Princess Vita and Prince Maxie,' Dad said, putting a finger to my lips.

I didn't say any more. I held it in all through tea. Gran laid out turkey sandwiches and mince pies and chocolate log.

'Now for pity's sake go easy, Em. Maybe you'd be better off with plain bread and butter,' said Gran.

I was feeling so empty I was ready to wolf everything down. The food tasted strange though, too light, like cotton wool. My head felt stuffed with cotton wool too. I couldn't think properly. It was just like a dream. Here I was, licking chocolate off my fingers, having my Christmas tea, and Vita and Maxie were pretending to feed Dancer and being all giggly and silly—but Mum was upstairs in her room, not having any tea at all.

Gran tried taking her a tray but she brought it back down untouched.

'I want Mum,' Maxie said suddenly, sliding off his chair.

'No, leave her alone, Maxie, she's got a bad headache,' said Gran.

'She gave *me* a bad headache with all that shouting,' said Vita. Then she paused. 'She is OK now though, isn't she, Dad?'

'I think she still feels a bit poorly, Princess,' said Dad.

'No wonder,' Gran spat out. 'You lying pig.'

'Now, now. Come on. You were the one who told me to think of the kids. We don't want to spoil their Christmas,' said Dad.

He tried very hard, dancing and singing and playing jokes. When Vita got over-excited and Maxie got tearful he squashed up on the sofa with them and made Dancer tell them a long story about her little reindeerhood in Lapland. Santa came on a talent-spotting visit when the reindeer school had its sports day. Dancer ran like the wind and won her race even though she was the youngest reindeer and her antlers were still as small and furry as pussy willow.

I wanted to snuggle up and listen too but I crept

34

out of the room, past Gran angrily washing the tea things in the kitchen, up the stairs to Mum. I listened outside her room, scared of going in, feeling weird and embarrassed. Then I heard her little sobs, just like Maxie's, and I went rushing in to her. She still had all her clothes on but she was right under the duvet, hunched up in a soggy ball.

'Oh Mum, don't cry so,' I said. I burrowed under the covers and put my arms tight round her as if she was my little girl and I was her mother.

'What am I going to do, Em?' she sobbed. 'I can't live without him.'

'It's OK, Mum, it's OK,' I said over and over, trying to soothe her.

She wriggled away from me, suddenly furious. 'It's not badword OK, you silly little girl. He's leaving us for another woman, for God's sake,' Mum hissed.

'No he's not. He's fine now, Mum. He's being really lovely to Vita and Maxie and me. He's trying to make it up to us. He won't go, not really. He *loves* us.'

'Did he say he wasn't going?'

I swallowed. 'Yes,' I said, because I so wanted it to be true.

Mum held onto me. 'You're sure?'

'Well . . .'

Mum knew I wasn't sure but she badly wanted it to be true too. She let me convince her.

'I'll find it hard to forgive him, though,' she said. 'This isn't the first time, Em. There are things you don't know about him. I don't know why I'm so desperate to hold onto him. I'd maybe be better off without him, without all this uncertainty and heartbreak.'

35

'But you love him, Mum.'

'Of course I love him, Em.' Mum sat up and gave me a proper hug. Then she switched on her crystal-drop lamp and looked at herself in the mirror.

'God, what a sight I look!'

Mum's very pretty but she really did look a sight, even in the soft sparkly light of the lamp. Her hair was sticking up in clumps and her eyelids were sore and swollen, like purple grapes. Her dark lipstick was smeared all round her mouth, like Vita when she's been drinking Ribena.

'No wonder he's got sick of me,' Mum moaned.

'You go and wash your face and put lots of make-up on,' I said. 'Then you'll knock him dead.'

'OK, miss, I'll do as I'm told,' said Mum.

She got herself sorted and then slipped her feet back into her new silver sandals.

'My million-dollar mum,' I said.

'Oh, Em, you're the sweetest, weirdest kid,' said Mum, her face crumpling.

'Don't cry again, you'll mess up all your make-up!'

'OK, OK, I'm not crying,' said Mum, blinking like crazy.

We walked downstairs hand in hand. Gran came out into the hall holding a tea towel.

'God, you're going to beg him to stay, aren't you?' she said. 'You'll never learn, Julie. After the way he's treated you! He needs strangling.' She twisted the tea towel violently, as if it was Dad's neck.

Mum took no notice. She took a deep breath. She held it for a long moment, her chest high, her lips clamped together. Then she breathed out and

36

walked into the living room. Dad looked anxious as she swayed towards him in her silver sandals. Vita sat up straight, Dancer hanging limply from her arm. Maxie jammed his thumb in his mouth and hunched up very small, as if he was trying to make himself invisible.

'Hello, darlings,' Mum said, brightly and bravely. She stretched and yawned, acting like she'd just woken up. 'Mm, I had a lovely nap. Shall we see what's on telly now?'

She wasn't really kidding anyone, not even Maxie, but we all acted like we hadn't heard any of the shouting and sobbing.

Dad gently pushed Vita along the sofa and patted the cushion. 'Come and sit down, babe,' he said gently.

Mum sat beside him. Vita, Maxie and I arranged ourselves round them. Gran sat sniffing and sighing in her chair opposite. We watched all the Christmas specials on the television and whenever there was a funny bit we all laughed a little too hilariously. Maxie snorted so much that he gave himself hiccups.

'You're getting over-tired, young man. Time you were in bed,' said Gran.

'No no no!' Maxie squealed.

'Yes yes yes!' said Dad. 'Hey, Maxie, Dancer wants to tell you about her reindeer house back in Lapland. You'll never guess what sort of bed she has.'

Maxie let Dad carry him upstairs. Vita started clamouring, so Dad carried her on his other arm. I watched, wishing I could whittle myself down to pocket size so I could cling to Dad like a little monkey too. I clumped along behind them instead.

Dad invented an entire Lapland saga, telling us about the baby reindeer nurseries with their green mossy cots with swan's-down quilts, and then describing reindeer school, where they had lessons in dancing, trotting, galloping, and special flying instruction for advanced and extra-talented reindeer.

Maxie fell asleep first. Dad tucked him under his own blankets and and ruffled his dark tufty hair. Vita allowed herself to be tucked up too, but was clearly willing herself to stay awake, her forehead furrowed with the effort of keeping her eyes wide open. But eventually she gave a little sigh, clasped Dancer to her chest, and fell asleep too.

Dad wriggled his hand free of the glove puppet and patted Vita gently on her bony shoulder. She'd refused to put on her own Barbie pyjamas and was wearing one of Mum's little black nightie tops. We'd argued over which one of us would wear it when Mum broke one of the straps and donated it to our dressing-up box. I won, but when I tried it on Vita laughed cruelly and said I looked like one of the hippos in her Disney video. I shoved her hard in the chest and said she was just jealous, but I let her commandeer the little black nightie after that. Vita looked wonderful in it, like a little midnight fairy.

'My girlie,' Dad whispered, and he kissed her high forehead.

The room seemed very quiet. Dad smiled at me, not quite meeting my eyes.

'Into bed, Princess Emerald,' he said.

'Dad?'

'Now come on, darling, it's way past your bed time.'

'Dad, promise you'll stay?'

Dad screwed up his face for a moment. Then he stood up, seized my hand and kissed my ring. 'Your wish is my command, Princess Emerald,' he said. 'Now stop looking so worried and hip-hop into bed.'

Dad started a hip-hop little song about Princess Em and her magic ring, bling bling. I sang along too. I even danced round the bed, but when Dad tried to tuck the duvet under my chin I flung my arms round his neck.

'Hey, hey, you're throttling me!' Dad joked.

'Dad, you do promise, don't you?'

'Play another tune, Princess,' said Dad. 'I said that your wish is my command, don't you remember?'

'You didn't actually *say* you promised. Say it, Dad. *Please* say it.'

'OK, OK. I promise.'

'You promise you'll stay for ever?'

'I promise I'll stay for ever,' he said. 'Now give me a kiss night-night. You never know, you might just transform me from a loathsome toad into a handsome prince.'

'You're a handsome prince already, silly,' I said, kissing him.

*   *   *

I was wrong. He was a total toad.

I woke early, my heart beating fast. I slid out of bed and crept across the carpet, not wanting to wake Vita or Maxie. I padded down the hall. I listened outside Mum and Dad's door. I heard muffled sobs. I ran into the bedroom. Mum was sitting on the edge of the bed, rocking backwards and forwards, her hands tugging her hair.

Dad had broken his promise. He'd gone already.

Three

Dad left me a note. I can't quite remember what it said. Something about not wanting to upset me. He'd drawn a little toad where he signed his name. He'd even taken the trouble to colour it with Maxie's new felt tips.

I didn't want the others to see it. I smoothed it out carefully and tucked it underneath my jumper, next to my heart. The paper tickled a little but I didn't mind.

When I was helping Gran mash the potatoes for our cold turkey lunch she suddenly cocked her head on one side.

'What's that crackling, Em?' she asked.

'Nothing,' I said quickly, mashing harder.

'You've got something stuffed down your jumper! For heaven's sake, you're not padding your vest with tissues and pretending you've got breasts, are you?'

'No!' I said, folding my arms across my chest and blushing violently.

'Don't be so *daft*, Em,' said Gran, her fingers scrabbling under my jumper.

43

'Don't! Get off me!' I said.

I couldn't stop her. She felt the letter. It tore right across as she dragged it free.

'My letter! Now look what you've done,' I shouted. 'You've torn it.'

Gran was holding the letter at arm's length, as if it was dripping with something disgusting. 'I'm glad I've torn it!' She said. 'I'm going to tear it into tiny shreds.' She tore and tore, little particles of paper flying everywhere.

I couldn't grab it back in time. I watched, weeping.

'You can stop that silly noise too. We've had enough weeping and wailing going on, enough tears to sink the *Titanic*. If you ask me I think you should be shedding tears of joy to be rid of that two-timing conniving Mr Smoothie. I never liked him right from the day your mother brought him home. I said as much too, but she didn't listen to me. She never does. No one in this house ever listens to what I say.'

I put my hands over my ears to show her I wasn't listening either. I certainly wasn't going to help her mash the potatoes. It didn't matter anyway. None of us ate much lunch. Even Vita turned up her nose at potatoes. She didn't eat anything at all. Maxie just had pudding. Mum drank a whole bottle of wine but had nothing to eat.

I said I wasn't hungry either and went without. Then halfway through the long long afternoon I crept into the kitchen and started pulling little shreds off the turkey. Once I'd started I couldn't stop. I tore at the turkey, tearing off great strips, so hungry I wanted to gnaw at it like a dog.

I heard footsteps and leaped back, guiltily wiping

my greasy hands on my skirt, waiting for Gran to give me another lecture on my greediness. It wasn't Gran, thank goodness, it was Vita. She had Dancer on her hand, the brown fur reaching all the way up her bony little arm almost to her armpit.

'Hi, you,' I said, tearing off another piece of turkey.

Vita's eyes widened. 'Gran will go bananas if she sees you doing that!'

'I don't care. I hate Gran,' I said fiercely.

Vita blinked. Then she wiped her nose with one of Dancer's antlers. 'I hate her too,' she said.

'No you don't,' I said. 'You like her heaps. You're her favourite. She's always giving you treats and letting you get away with stuff, you know she is.'

'She's horrid though. She says Dad's gone away with another lady and he's not ever coming back. She's telling lies, isn't she, Em?'

'What did Mum say?'

'She just cried more and said she didn't know. She told me to go away because she's got an awful headache. Maxie says he's got a headache too. He's mad, he's gone to bed and it's only the afternoon. It's gone all weird and horrid and upside down. Gran told me to play a game but I want to play games with *Dad*.' Tears started dribbling down Vita's cheeks. 'Em, *is* he coming back?'

'Of course he is. In a bit. He wouldn't go away for good without telling us. He's *got* to come back to see us. Even *my* dad came back to see me when I was little before Mum told him to get lost.'

'I can't remember your dad,' said Vita.

'I can't remember him either,' I said. It wasn't quite true. I still had nightmares about him. I

45

shivered, and stuffed more turkey in my mouth.

Vita looked at me. 'Our dad won't go scary like yours, will he?' she asked.

'No, of course not, Vita. Dad couldn't *ever* be scary, you know that.'

'And he will come back?' Vita said, Dancer drooping down her arm.

I wiped my hands properly and then commandeered Dancer, fitting her over my fist.

'Hello, Princess Vita,' I made her say, copying Dad's voice for her, all funny and fruity. 'Now listen here, my dear, no one knows you dad better than I do. I say he's absolutely definitely coming back.'

'Now? Today?'

'Maybe not today.'

'Tomorrow?'

'Mm, perhaps. Oooh, just look at that scrumptious plate of turkey! I'm feeling very peckish, Princess Vita. Hint hint!'

Vita laughed and pretended to feed her, but she wouldn't be distracted. 'Dad will come back *soon*, won't he?'

'Yes, yes, my dear, Dad won't let us down. He'll come back as soon as he can. Tell you what, let's use a little turkey magic.' I made Dancer circle the turkey plate, prancing round and round, while I pulled more meat off with my free hand.

'I don't want to eat any turkey,' said Vita.

'No, no, I'm just looking for— Aha!' I scrabbled away at the turkey, tugging at a little twig of bone. I wriggled it free and then gave it to Dancer. She held it out triumphantly.

'What have I found, Princess Vita?' said Dancer.

'A bone?' said Vita doubtfully.

46

'A *wish*bone! You take one end, hooking your little finger round it, OK? Princess Emerald will take hold of the other end. Then when I say so, you both pull, and the Princess who gets the longest piece of bone has a magic wish.'

'That's not fair!' wailed Vita, poking Dancer as if she was a real person. 'Em's bigger and stronger than me so she'll get the turkey wish.'

'What will she wish for, Princess Poke-and-Prod?' said Dancer.

Vita thought about it. 'Ah!' she said. 'But I still wish *I* could do the wishing.'

'That's one wish wasted already,' said Dancer. 'Now quit prodding me, missy, or I'll stick my antlers up your nose.'

Vita started giggling.

'Come on, Vita, pull the wishbone,' I said, thrusting it at her.

She pulled. I pulled. I twisted the wishbone a little, applying more pressure. I knew we were going to wish identical wishes but I was just like Vita. *I* wanted to make the wish.

The wishbone shattered. Vita was left holding a tiny stump. I had almost the whole v-shaped bone in my hand.

'Ooh!' said Vita. 'Go on, then, Em. Wish. Wish it *hard*.'

I hung onto the wishbone, and shut my eyes. I wished for Dad to come back. I wished it so fiercely I felt my head would burst. I wished and wished and wished.

'Em, you've gone purple,' said Vita.

I opened my eyes and breathed out, exhausted.

'Will it come true?' said Vita, glancing at the door, expecting Dad to bound in right that minute.

'It *will* come true, but maybe not for a little while,' I said.

Vita sighed. She looked at Dancer. 'Can't *you* make it come true, as quick as quick?' she said.

I found I was looking at Dancer too, even though my own hand was up inside her. She nodded her head. She shook her head. Nod, shake, nod, shake.

'Quick as quick or slow as slow,' she said enigmatically. 'Quick quick *slow slow*, quick quick *slow*, like the ballroom dance, my dear.'

I seized Vita and quick-stepped her round her kitchen, Dancer holding her round the waist.

*　　　*　　　*

It wasn't quick quick. We waited the day after Boxing Day. Then the day after and the day after and the day after and the day after. Mum got up off her bed and went out looking for him—all over his favourite places in town, even up to London and back. She phoned his mobile again and again but it was always switched off. She tried phoning all his mates. She went down to the Pink Palace where they both worked even though she knew it was all shut up until after the New Year. She wandered round and round all day, wearing the silver sandals, as if she thought they might walk her directly to Dad. Her feet were rubbed raw by the time she limped home and she'd lost the tip of one stiletto heel.

'Don't cry, Mum, you can take them to Mr Minit,' I said. 'They're not badly broken.'

'Yes they are,' said Vita. 'Can I have them for dressing up, Mum?'

48

'*I* want them, Mum,' said Maxie, sticking his fat little feet inside the sandals and shuffling across the room.

'Get them shoes off, sharpish,' said Gran. 'Boys don't wear high heels. I don't know why you're all fighting over them. They belong in the bin with all the rest of the trash.'

'They're beautiful shoes,' said Mum, snatching them from Maxie and cradling them as if they were silver dolls.

'Yes, cost a fortune, like the rest of Frankie's ridiculous Christmas presents. *Whose* fortune, Julie? I bet he paid with your joint credit card. You'll be paying off your own presents until *next* Christmas. And what about all the money I've lent him, my savings from slaving in that blooming office? What about the kids? Is he just going to walk out of their lives without paying a penny in child support? You're rubbish at choosing men— one violent nutter, one sleazy charmer—'

'You're rubbish at men too, Gran,' I said furiously, because she was making Mum cry. 'Grandad cleared off ages ago.'

'Good riddance! Catch me making a fool of myself a second time,' said Gran, sniffing. 'I don't know why you're in such a state, Julie. You knew what he was like. Why do you have to let him hurt you so? You need to toughen up a bit.'

Gran seized hold of Mum as if she was personally going to shake some sense into her—but then her arms went right round her. Gran held Mum and rocked her. Mum howled. Vita and Maxie went and joined in the hug too.

I stayed separate, picking up Dancer from the floor. We went out into the kitchen together and

49

had a sneaky snack from the larder. Dancer decided to try a raisin or two out of the packet, and then she couldn't seem to stop. She liked the icing sugar too, because it reminded her of snow.

'Snow snow, thick thick snow,' I murmured, doing the wishing dance round and round the kitchen table.

Then I heard a mobile ringing. It was Mum's mobile in her handbag, where she'd dropped it in the hallway. I dashed to answer it. It could be any of Mum's mates but I knew it was Dad, I just *knew* it.

'Hello, Julie?'

'Oh, Dad, Dad, Dad!' I said.

'Em! Hello, sweetheart! How are you, babe? How's everyone? Can I speak to your mum in a minute?'

Mum was already in the hall, on her knees beside me, trying to snatch the phone away. I hung onto it.

'Dad, when are you coming back?' I asked.

'Well, I'm planning to come and see you New Year's Day. I thought we could have a fun day out, you, me, Vita and Maxie, right?'

'Oh yes, *please*!' I said.

'What? Is he really coming back? Give me my phone, Em!' Mum said. She prised my fingers off it and listened herself.

'*I* want to talk to Dad! I must talk to him. I've got heaps and heaps to tell him,' said Vita.

'And me! I want to! Let *me*!' Maxie shrieked.

Mum sat still, staring straight ahead as if she was looking right through us.

'Mum?' I whispered.

She didn't seem to hear. She didn't react to

Vita's imperious commands or Maxie's whines. She just knelt there, as if she was praying. Then she suddenly pressed the little red button, cutting Dad off.

'Mum!' we wailed.

'Good for you, Julie,' said Gran, watching from the living-room doorway.

'What is it, Mum? Why won't you speak to Dad?' I asked, stunned.

'You're the meanest mum *ever*. You didn't let me even say hello!' Vita wept.

'I want Dad!' Maxie bawled. 'Make Dad come back, Mum!'

'Stop it!' said Mum. She staggered to her feet. 'I can't *make* Dad come back.'

'He said he's coming on New Year's Day. He said it, he really did. He's coming back then,' I said.

'No. He's coming to take you three out. But he's not coming back to live here. He's making that quite plain. He's still with this woman.'

'You don't *know* that, Mum.'

'Yes I do. I heard her whispering to him,' said Mum.

'He's still going to take us out though?' said Vita.

'I don't know. I suppose so,' said Mum.

'Oh whoopee!' said Vita tactlessly. She started dancing up and down the hall.

'Dad's coming, Dad's coming!' Maxie yelled, galloping after her.

Mum stared at them. I didn't know what to say, what to do. Most of me wanted to dance too, because I so wanted a day out with Dad, no matter what. But he clearly wasn't inviting Mum. It would be so awful for her stuck at home with Gran.

51

I knew I should tell her that I didn't want to go. He wasn't even my own dad after all. But I couldn't bear to miss seeing him.

'I'll have to go to look after Vita and Maxie,' I said. 'You know what they're like, how silly they get. Dad's not always good at getting them to behave.'

Mum looked at me. She didn't say anything. The look was enough.

Gran seized hold of Vita and Maxie, giving them both a little shake. 'Stop that silly shrieking,' she said crossly. 'Don't go getting your hopes up. I don't think your dad will even bother to turn up.'

*   *   *

It looked as if Gran was right.

I was up very very very early on January 1st. We hadn't stayed up on New Year's Eve. Even Mum and Gran went to bed way before twelve. *Last* New Year's Eve we'd had a little party and Dad had bought a bottle of champagne. He gave me a tiny glassful and Vita and Maxie a few sips. Maxie rolled round the carpet afterwards, playing at being drunk, while Vita and I danced with Dad.

I tossed and turned half the night, thinking about Dad drinking and dancing with this horrible Sarah instead of us. I decided that Vita and Maxie and I had to be on our very best behaviour so that Dad would realize he couldn't bear to be without us.

I had a bath and washed my hair and then brushed it all out very carefully. I hoped Mum would loop up little plaity pieces at the sides and tie a velvet ribbon on for me, so that Dad would call me his pretty princess. I put on my best party outfit, a tight sparkly top and velvet trousers.

Then I looked in the mirror and took them off again. The top was way too tight now and the seams of the velvet trousers were nearly splitting. I didn't look like a pretty princess, I looked more like a pot-bellied pig. I stood in my knickers, sorting through all the clothes in my wardrobe, nearly weeping. Maxie stayed huddled up in his bear cave but Vita woke up and watched me.

'Put something *on*, Em,' she said.

'I haven't *got* anything,' I snivelled. 'All my clothes look rubbish. Correction. *I* look rubbish.'

'Yeah, well, we all know that,' said Vita. She stretched smugly. '*I'm* going to wear my disco-dancing queen outfit.'

I glared at her. Dad bought Vita this ultra-tight sparkly fancy-dress outfit for her last birthday. It had a halter top and low-slung trousers. They showed off Vita's tiny waist and totally flat stomach.

Vita was obviously thinking this too. 'I'm going to draw a special tummy tattoo with felt tips.'

'Not *my* felt tips,' Maxie mumbled from under his covers. 'I'm going to wear my cowboy outfit with Dad's cowboy boots. He left them in his wardrobe—I looked.'

'You can't wear Dad's boots, you'll fall over,' I said.

'Me can, me can, me can,' Maxie insisted.

'Quit that baby talk, Maxie, you're pathetic,' I said.

I tried on every single outfit in my wardrobe but they all looked awful. I seemed to have expanded horrifically overnight. I ended up wearing my Miss

Kitty nightie over my loosest jeans. I hoped it looked like a smock top. I wondered about borrowing a pair of Mum's heels seeing as Maxie was helping himself to Dad's cowboy boots.

'For pity's sake, you look like a circus,' said Gran, when we came down to the kitchen. She was making our usual holiday breakfast—boiled eggs and soldiers. 'You needn't think you're going out like that. Take those ludicrous boots back at once, Maxie. Vita, you look like a little tart, take that horrible outfit *off*. And what are you playing at, Em, wearing your *nightie*? You're old enough to know better. You should set your little brother and sister an example, not egg them on all the time.'

'Egg, egg, egg!' Maxie shouted, bashing the top of his boiled egg so hard that yoke spurted everywhere.

'I don't!' I said, taking Maxie's spoon away. 'That's so mean, Gran. I try to make Vita and Maxie behave, don't I, Mum?'

Mum was sitting at the kitchen table sipping black coffee and smoking. She'd got up even earlier than me. She was in *her* prettiest clothes, a fluffy blue sweater and her embroidered jeans. She'd even painted her toenails silver to match her sandals.

She smiled anxiously at me, flicking her ash. 'Yes, you're a good kid, Em. Quit nagging her, Mum.'

'OK, I'll start in on you, Julie. Why in God's name are you smoking again when you gave it up years ago? Are you mad? Well yes, obviously you are, because you're all dressed up like a dog's dinner to see this pig husband of yours, when I wouldn't mind betting he won't turn up. Even if he

54

does, he's not taking *you* out, he's made that plain.'

'Do you ever listen to yourself, Mum? Do you get a kick out of saying hurtful things? I can't stop you saying stuff to me, but I'm certainly not going to have you being mean to the kids, especially not now their whole world's been turned upside down. Take no notice of your gran, kids, you wear what you like. I think you all look lovely.'

I nodded at Gran triumphantly but I couldn't really enjoy the victory. I knew Maxie really did look silly in his cowboy outfit. Dad's boots were so big they came right up to his bottom. Vita looked drop-dead gorgeous but like she was part of a dancing competition, not dressed to go out for the day. And though I kept hoping my Miss Kitty top looked perfectly OK, it was starting to look more and more like my nightie.

Still, Mum styled my hair for me and gave me my velvet ribbon. She tied another in Vita's wispy locks too, and she gelled Maxie's black mop so that it stuck up and looked very cute.

Then we waited. And waited and waited and waited. Mum had endless cups of coffee and cigarettes. I started secretly chomping chocolate biscuits because I felt so empty. I tried to keep Vita and Maxie amused, making Dancer draw her Santa experiences with Maxie's felt pens, but I didn't have a clue what a sleigh looked like and I was rubbish at drawing reindeer too.

I found it hard to concentrate because I was straining to hear Dad's footsteps walking up our path. I kept thinking I heard him and went running, but each time there was no one on the doorstep.

'I told you, he's not coming,' said Gran.

I wanted to punch her. Mum looked like she

55

did too.

'Give him a chance, Mum. He's not late. He didn't say a specific time, he just said he'd pop over to collect the kids in the morning.'

'It's quarter to twelve, Julie.'

'It's still technically morning.'

'And you're technically a gullible mug, getting yourself all worked up over that loser. Look at the state of you—*and* the kids.'

'Stop getting at our mum and being so mean about our dad!' I said fiercely. 'You're not supposed to talk like that in front of children.'

'Children aren't supposed to talk back to their grandmas like that, you cheeky little madam,' said Gran. 'Em? Em, I'm talking to you!'

I wasn't listening. I heard footsteps. I ran. This time I was right!

'Dad!'

I threw myself at him, my arms round his neck. He hadn't shaved so his chin was scratchy and his hair was tousled round his shoulders like he'd just got out of bed but I didn't care.

'Daddy, oh, my daddy!' Vita cried, copying the girl in *The Railway Children* video.

Dad scooped her up in his arms.

'D-a-d!' Maxie bellowed, butting Dad so hard with his gelled head that we nearly all toppled over.

'Hey, kids, calm down!' said Dad.

He stopped, swallowing, rubbing the space between his eyebrows as he looked the length of the hall to where Mum was standing. 'Hi, Julie,' he said softly, as if they'd only just met.

Mum didn't say anything. She had her arms tightly folded, her hands gripping her elbows.

'It's OK for me to take the kids out?' said Dad.

56

'Can't Mum come too?' I begged.

Dad hesitated. 'Well . . . this is a day out just for us,' he said.

Mum turned on her heel, walked into the kitchen and shut the door.

'Oh God. Julie? Look, OK, you come too, if you really want to. We have to talk, I know that. I just didn't want any hassle, it's not fair on the kids,' said Dad.

'How dare you!' said Gran.

'Oh God, I'm not up to this,' said Dad. 'Come on, kids, let's get cracking.' He took hold of Vita's and Maxie's hands and started pulling them out the door.

'Dad! Wait! They haven't got their coats. And Maxie can't walk in your boots,' I said, scrabbling around on the pegs for our three coats and kicking my way through old wellies and slippers for Maxie's shoes.

'You're like a little mum, Em. More grown up than the lot of us,' said Dad.

My heart thumped with pride under my Miss Kitty nightie. We followed Dad out of the house, half in and half out of our coats, Maxie scuffling in his unlaced shoes. We didn't say goodbye to Gran. We didn't even say goodbye to Mum.

Four

Dad took us on the train up to London. He bought a takeaway cup of black coffee at the station, and a bag of doughnuts for us. He shuddered when I offered him our bag of sugary doughnuts.

'Go on, Dad, they're delicious,' I said, biting a doughnut until the scarlet jam spurted out.

'Look, I've got lipstick,' said Vita, smearing jam round her mouth.

'Me too, me too,' said Maxie.

'I'm not very hungry, Em. You guys eat them,' said Dad.

'Don't you feel well, Dad?' I asked sympathetically.

'I'm fine,' said Dad, shivering. He pulled my woolly scarf tight round his neck. 'Ooh, what a great cosy scarf this is!'

Dad had a little sleep on the train. Vita kept wanting to wake him up and Maxie started clamouring, 'Are we in London yet?' two minutes after we got on the train, but I managed to distract them. We looked out the window at people's back gardens, playing Hunt the Child, on the lookout for swings and sandpits and bikes and balls.

Vita and Maxie kept squabbling over who saw things first. I kept glancing at Dad. He was very pale, huddled over, frowning in his sleep. I wondered if he was dreaming about us. I wanted to whisper in his ear, hypnotizing him when he was unconscious. *You are going to come back home, Dad. You love Mum and Vita and Maxie and me. You can't live without us.*

I shook his arm gently when we got to Waterloo. Dad opened his eyes and looked startled, as if he'd forgotten all about us. Then he smiled. He went to the gents at the station and came back looking a bit better, his face washed, his breath minty.

'Right, my darlings, we're off to the parade,' he said.

He told us this was a special New Year's Day parade. We had to walk there because Maxie was terrified of the escalators in the tube station. Dad kept making up stories about the parade, until he had Vita and Maxie believing there would be bareback riders in sparkly bikinis on snow-white horses and painted elephants with jewelled tusks and winged monkeys flying right over people's heads and snatching their hats off.

I knew he was making it all up but I almost believed it too, so the real parade was a disappointment. We couldn't see properly for a start because there were such crowds. Dad let Vita and Maxie take turns sitting on his shoulder. I was much too big. If I stood on tiptoe I could see the heads of lots and lots of chanting girls. Every now and then they threw sticks in the air or waved feathers, but that was all. There were big floats with famous people dressed up, waving and calling, but mostly we couldn't work out who they were.

Maxie whined whenever he had to let Vita have a turn on Dad's shoulders, so I tried picking him up.

'Lift me higher, Em, *higher*!' Maxie yelled. 'I can't see a sausage.'

Then, very spookily, a giant walking sausage came bobbing along as if Maxie had rubbed a magic lamp and conjured it up. It was part of a troupe of people advertising a new breakfast show on television. Men dressed up as eggs, bacon, cups of tea and packets of cornflakes were also parading along, having to take mincing little steps because of their big polystyrene costumes. The Sausage didn't really look like an obvious sausage when it was separated from its breakfast companions. Lots of people were falling about laughing, thinking it was something very rude.

I hitched Maxie too high. He saw the Sausage. He screamed.

'A monster! A monster! A big pink monster's coming to get me!'

The crowd collapsed, not taking Maxie's terror seriously.

'Hey, Maxie, it's just a big sausage,' Dad said. 'Don't be frightened, sweetheart. The sausage should be frightened of you. You could take a big bite and eat it all up.'

Maxie was yelling too loudly to listen to Dad. He probably wouldn't have believed him anyway.

'We've got to get out of here, Dad,' I said.

'How?' said Dad, because we were all hemmed in, barely able to breathe.

Maxie showed us how. He paused in mid scream, shuddered—and then was horribly sick all over me.

The crowd parted as if by magic and Dad led us through. I was weeping now as well as Maxie. Vita started crying too, so as not to be left out.

Dad stared at us helplessly. He tried dabbing at Maxie and me with a tissue but it was hopeless. The sick was even in my *hair*.

'You'll have to go into a ladies and wash it in the basin. You'll have to help her, Vita,' said Dad.

'Yuck, I'm not touching all their sick. Anyway, I don't know *how* to wash hair, Mum does mine,' said Vita. 'You two are disgusting. *I'm* never sick.'

'*I* wasn't sick,' I sobbed.

'You were at Christmas,' said Vita.

'That's enough, Vita,' said Dad. He was starting to look very queasy himself.

'The pink monster, the pink monster, it's coming to get me!' Maxie yelled.

'For God's sake, Maxie, we're miles away from the stupid sausage. It wasn't a monster, it was just a poor out-of-work actor just like Daddy in a manky costume. Maxie, *I've* dressed up in daft costumes. I was once a chicken in a shopping centre when a new cheapo chicken restaurant opened up. All these little kids kept barging into me going *cluck cluck cluck.*'

'He's not listening, Dad,' I said, wriggling. 'Ugh, it's all soggy round my neck. I can't stand this.'

'Here, we'll take your coat off,' said Dad, helping me out of it at arm's length. 'Oh Lord, it's all on your nightie thingy too. Perhaps we could buy you a new top or jacket or something and stick these stinky ones in a carrier bag? Where does Mum buy your clothes, Em?'

'I don't know,' I said.

It was hard to find clothes that would fit me in

ordinary places like Tammy or The Gap, but I didn't want Dad to know that. Gran had once sent off for a Big Kiddo catalogue and I nearly died, because they were all clothes specially for fat kids. I *knew* I was a fat kid but I didn't want the labels on my clothes reminding me all the time.

'We'll try to clean you up a bit and then take you to one of the big posh shops. They'll have a special girls' department, Em, all sorts,' said Dad.

I guessed he meant all *sizes*. I nodded at him gratefully for his tact, though I could feel myself going bright pink.

'It's not fair!' Vita wailed inevitably. '*I* want new clothes if Em's getting them. It's not my fault that Maxie wasn't sick on me! *Please* can I have new clothes, Dad? I need a new sparkly top and some of those shiny trousers with lots of pockets and there's these pink and purple trainers with glitter on the edgy bit, they're sooo cool.'

'OK, OK, little Vita Fashionista,' said Dad. 'I'll do you a deal. Get Maxie to shut up and I'll buy you *all* a new outfit.'

I stared at Dad anxiously. I knew he didn't have any money. I'd heard Gran going on about it bitterly enough times. But I couldn't stay wearing the sick-stained stuff. I badly wanted Dad to get us all new clothes. I didn't protest.

It was a waste of time anyway. All the shops we saw were shut.

'Oh God, what are we going to do now?' said Dad. 'Look at you, Em, you're shivering. You'll catch your death of cold without your coat. Maybe we'd better take you straight home.'

'No!' Vita wailed. 'No, no, no! We're having a whole day out with you, Dad. Just send Em home!'

65

'Yeah, just send Em,' said Maxie.

'That's so mean, Maxie! It's all your fault, not mine!' I protested.

'Ssh, ssh, OK! We won't send anybody home,' said Dad. 'I know what we'll do. We'll go to *my* home.'

We all stared at him. What did he mean, *his* home? It sounded much too permanent.

It wasn't his home. It was Sarah's.

We went on the Underground.

'You'll have to put up with it, Maxie, we've no other way of getting there,' said Dad. 'Come on, be a man.'

Maxie couldn't even manage being a little boy. He whimpered like a baby. Dad picked him up and carried him. Maxie moaned when the tube thundered into the station. He burrowed right inside Dad's jacket, using his scarf as a cuddle blanket.

I sat, stiff and sodden and smelly, while everyone kept their distance and stared. Vita was the only member of our family looking normal. She sat demurely, smiling up at strangers, while they put their heads on one side and purred at her.

I wished I was Vita. I always always always wished I was Vita.

When we were out of the Underground at last she put her hand confidently into Dad's.

'Is your house a nice house, Dad?'

'Well, it isn't exactly *my* house, Princess Vita. Now, there's a thing. If I had my magic house it would be like a fairy castle and it would have four turrets and you could have one turret all to yourself. You'd go up all these windy stairs, carpeted in deep pink, with pale-pink walls

66

patterned with bluebirds and butterflies, and then right at the top there would be this wooden door carved with hearts and flowers and inside would be your own special room.'

'Can it be pink too?'

'The pinkest pink ever. You'd have a pink four-poster bed with rose-pink velvet curtains and a patchwork quilt in every shade of pink with little red hearts stitched into the centre of each patch.'

'Where will Dancer sleep?'

'Oh, Dancer's got her own sleigh-shaped wooden bed. We'll hang a little bell mobile above it so that as it spins it tinkles softly, so she can dream she's back with Santa.'

'Um, you said a rude word,' Maxie said, still clutching Dad about the neck, his skinny legs wound round his waist. 'They say tinkle at nursery when you need to do a wee. Dad, I need to do a wee now.'

'Well, hold it for a bit, son.'

'I can't,' said Maxie, wriggling.

'You'd better! We've had enough contact with your bodily fluids to last a lifetime,' said Dad. 'Haven't we, Princess Emerald? OK, shall we do your turret now?'

'No, me, me!' said Maxie. 'I want my own turret, for me and all my bears.'

'Indeed, you can have a veritable bear lair and we'll make sure there are pots of honey and spoons, all sizes, only *you* get a great big giant vat of honey and a ladle and you can go lick lick lick until you're sticky all over. Then you can go to your very own indoor paddling pool and splash around until you're squeaky clean and *then* . . . OK, what do you start doing then, Prince Maxie?'

67

'I start in again on the honey!' said Maxie, smacking his lips.

'You got it!' said Dad. He turned round awkwardly; still lumbered with Maxie. 'Oh, poor Em, you look so miserable. Don't worry, darling, we'll get you all cleaned up in just a tick, I promise. Now, let's start on your turret.'

I so wanted Dad to invent a beautiful turret for me, but I needed to ask something first.

'What about *your* turret, Dad?'

Dad missed a beat. He knew what I was getting at. Who was going to climb up to his turret and live with him? Was it going to be Mum . . . or this Sarah?

I had a picture of her in my mind. I'd watched old movies with Mum and Gran and seen all the soaps. I knew what bad women were like who stole men away from their families. They were blonde with scarlet lipstick and they wore tight clothes that showed off their figures. They laughed a lot and licked their red lips and crossed and uncrossed their legs. I knew I would hate her.

Dad stopped at a little parade of shops and went up to a battered door beside an Indian grocery.

'That's a *shop*, Dad,' said Vita.

'I live up above it. It's handy when we run out of bread or milk,' said Dad.

'I didn't know you could live above a shop,' said Maxie. He craned his neck, looking up, as if he expected Dad's bed to be rocking on the roof and his chair topping a chimney stack.

'It's inside, little pal. Just an ordinary flat,' said Dad, getting the door open and leading us inside.

The stairs were very dark and smelled of strange food.

68

'I don't like it,' Maxie wailed.

'I'm afraid you're just going to have to lump it,' Dad said gently.

'This is *your* flat, Dad?' said Vita, stopping on the stairs.

'Well, technically speaking, it's Sarah's,' said Dad.

Vita said nothing, but she reached out and slid her hand into mine. I squeezed it hard and she squeezed back. Then Dad was knocking on the door, although he had the key in his hand.

'Sarah, sweetheart! I've brought the kids back,' he called.

He unlocked the door and we stepped warily inside. There wasn't a hall. We were straight away in a living room, although there was a bed in one corner with someone huddled under the purple velvet quilt.

'Sarah,' Dad said.

She stirred but didn't come out from under the quilt.

'It's not bed time,' said Maxie.

'Perhaps she's ill,' said Vita.

'She's fine, kids. She's just sleeping,' said Dad. 'Sarah, wake up. I've brought the kids to meet you.' He reached under the quilt and gave her a little shake.

'Frankie?' she mumbled. Then she sat up straight. She wasn't wearing a nightie or pyjamas, just a little stripy vest. She was almost as small and skinny as Vita, with short black hair sticking straight up and dark eye make-up rings round her eyes. She had a bluebird tattooed on her bare shoulder and matching blue varnish on her tiny bitten nails.

She blinked at us, scratching her very short hair. Then she wrinkled her nose. 'Oh dear, Frankie, did you puke?'

'It's the kids. That's why we're here. Poor Em needs a bath.'

'I wasn't the one who was sick,' I said.

'But you *are* the one who needs a clean coat. Sarah, do you have anything you could lend Em?' Dad asked.

'Oh God, Frankie, I don't know. I expect so. Look, you kids hurry up and have your bath because *I* want one too.' She smiled at Dad. 'Make me a cup of coffee, eh?'

'Sure, darling,' said Dad.

We stared at her, outraged. What was she doing, ordering our dad around? She didn't seem *that* much older than me.

'Are you a girl or a lady?' Maxie asked.

'Neither,' said Sarah, reaching for a packet of cigarettes and lighting up. She saw me staring. 'What?' she said, sounding irritated.

I looked at Dad. He's always *hated* smoking. Mum told us she used to smoke twenty a day but she had to give them up when she met Dad. I remembered her chewing gum desperately for weeks.

'Our dad doesn't like cigarettes,' said Vita.

'Well, your dad doesn't have to smoke them. All the more for me, Em,' said Sarah.

'I'm not *Em*!' said Vita, amazed. 'I'm Vita!'

'Whatever,' said Sarah.

She didn't seem to care. She was acting as if we were three mangy mongrels making a mess in her flat. She couldn't be bothered working out which was which. She obviously just wanted us out again as soon as possible.

'Off you go and have your bath then, Em,' said Dad. 'Try not to use too much hot water, sweetheart, if Sarah wants a bath afterwards.'

I ran a *minute* bath, barely a couple of centimetres of hot water, peeled off my clothes and then clambered in. I felt like a big pink hippo trying to wallow in a small puddle. I washed as quickly as I could. I had to borrow a flannel. I hoped it was Dad's. It was weird seeing his toothbrush, his razor, his special black hairbrush on the windowsill. Sarah's eye make-up and black hair dye and funny cakes of soap with bits of petal stuck inside them were scattered all over the place. Her purple and black stripy tights dangled above me from a line across the bath. Her underwear hung there too, but I was trying hard not to look at the horrible wispy things.

I got out and inspected the towels dubiously. None of them looked very clean. The bathroom floor was all bitty too. It didn't look as if Sarah ever bothered to vacuum. I thought of Mum rushing around with her hoover every morning because she had to keep our part of the house pin-neat. Gran always expected everywhere to be spick and span.

I hastily rubbed myself dry and pulled on my own knickers and jeans and socks and shoes. I couldn't put my Miss Kitty nightie back on because it was all sicky round the neck. I didn't know what to do. I didn't want to go back into the main room half dressed.

Vita tapped on the door. 'Em, let me in.'

She was holding a black jumper and a denim jacket. 'They're *hers*,' she said. 'She says she needs them back again.'

71

'What does she think I'm going to do, keep them?' I hissed. 'I *hate* having to wear her horrid clothes.'

I pulled on the black jumper. Sarah was a grown-up and I was still a child but the jumper was skin-tight on me. I knew it showed off all my plump bits. I covered it up quickly with the denim jacket. Even that was way on the skimpy side.

I felt my eyes filling with tears. I blinked quickly, hoping Vita wouldn't see me being such a baby.

Vita did see, but she surprised me. She reached up on tiptoe and put her arms round me. 'It's all right, you look OK, Em,' she whispered.

I plucked at the tight jumper. 'How can she be so little when she's grown up? Vita, do you think she's pretty? Prettier than Mum?'

Vita shook her head so hard her neck clicked. 'No, I think she's *horrible.*'

'Ssh!'

'I don't care if she hears. What is Dad *doing* with her?'

I didn't have a clue. I went back into the main room, standing there self-consciously.

'Wow! You look fantastic, Em,' said Dad. Then he looked past me, at Sarah. 'OK, babe, your bath time now. Then we'll all go out and get a bite to eat, right?'

It wasn't right. It was horribly wrong. Vita could barely wait until Sarah was in the bathroom.

'We want it to be just *us*, Dad, you, me, Maxie and Em.'

'Oh, come on, sweetie,' Dad said.

'This is *our* day, Dad, specially for us,' said Vita.

'Can't it be for all of us?' said Dad, tickling Vita under the chin to try to make her smile.

Vita glared back at Dad, her pointy chin stuck in the air. 'No it can't!' she said. She clenched her fists and gave him a pretend punch.

'No, it can't!' Maxie copied, hitting out at Dad too. He didn't know how to pretend and hit Dad hard.

'Hey, hey!' Dad's voice went suddenly cold and cross.

Vita and Maxie stared at him, shocked. Dad didn't ever get cross.

'Now stop behaving like silly babies, the pair of you. I've been longing for you to meet Sarah and this is the perfect opportunity. She's very special to me.'

'She can't be *that* special, Dad. You've only been with her since Christmas,' I said.

'I've known Sarah for six months, Em,' Dad said quietly.

'You've known Mum years and years and years,' I said.

Dad sighed. 'I thought you'd understand, Em. Now come on, all of you, let's lighten up. Stop pouting at me, Vita. Maxie, don't you dare cry. I know you're all going to love Sarah when you get to know her.'

We didn't get to love Sarah. We loathed her.

We didn't get to go to McDonald's. We went to this posh Italian restaurant. Dad insisted on ordering a plate of spaghetti each for Vita and Maxie though I knew they wouldn't eat it all. Sarah didn't eat much of hers either, though she messed around with it a great deal, twirling bits round and round her fork and sucking up strands like a little kid. Dad laughed at her, but when I copied he told me to stop messing around and eat properly.

'Look, you've spilled spaghetti sauce all down Sarah's black sweater!' said Dad. 'Em? I'm talking to you.'

I didn't want to talk to him. I didn't dare take my eyes off my plate in case I burst out crying. Dad didn't seem to understand how much he'd upset me. He went back to chatting with Sarah. She snuggled right up to him and whispered in his ear. They were like two hateful kids at school ganging up on us.

I stared at my spaghetti until it blurred into wriggling orange worms. I twisted my emerald ring round and round my finger under the table. I wanted to twist it right off and drop it on the dirty floor. I decided I couldn't stand Dad any more.

We went for a walk in a park afterwards. It was cold and drizzling and I shivered in Sarah's skimpy jacket.

'Oh poor Princess Emerald, you've been fated to be frozen all day,' said Dad, and he wrapped his arms round me.

I held myself stiffly but he wouldn't give up. 'Let's thaw you out, my lovely,' he said, cuddling me close. Then he put his hands under my arms and whirled me round and round. Dad's slim and short and I'm shamefully big but he treated me like I was as light as a feather.

Then he held my hand and started telling me about Princess Emerald in Glacier Land. It seemed so real it truly felt as if we were wrapped in rich furs, gliding over shiny white ice, with polar bears lumbering past, seals barking and waving their flippers, and penguins sliding comically on their tummies down the icy slopes into the black sea. My heart melted in this freezing fantasy land and in

74

two minutes I loved Dad so much I was willing to forgive him anything.

I even tried to be polite to Sarah. She didn't try to be polite to any of us. She walked along hunched up, her arms wrapped tight round her chest. Maxie tried to run after some ducks and tripped and fell headlong. Sarah didn't unwrap her arms even then. She simply stood still, waiting for someone else to pick him up and comfort him.

Dad mopped him up and then gave him a piggyback. Vita stalked along by herself, muttering to Dancer.

I tried to walk in step with Sarah.

'So where did you meet my dad?' I asked.

'Oh, around,' said Sarah, infuriatingly vague.

'Do you work at the Palace?'

'No, no.'

'So what work do you do?'

'I'm an actress.'

'So what have you been in?'

'This and that.'

I nodded. Dad usually said that too. It meant nothing very much at all recently.

'Vita wants to be an actress,' I said.

Vita heard and gave a little twirl.

'Yes, she would,' said Sarah. 'Do you want to be an actress too?'

I wondered if she was mocking me. 'I don't know what I want to be,' I said.

'Well, what are you good at?' said Sarah.

I thought hard. I started to panic. I wasn't really good at anything. I could make up stories but that didn't really count. My stories weren't anywhere near as good as Dad's, anyway. I liked colouring in my books but I was rubbish at drawing my own

75

people. I liked dancing when I was all by myself but I'd never been taught. I'd have died if I'd had to wear one of those skimpy little leotards.

'I'm not good at anything,' I said, sighing.

'Yes, you are. Em's good at looking after us,' said Vita, glancing over her shoulder.

Sarah didn't look impressed. 'Do you *like* looking after people?' she said.

I thought about it. I wasn't really that good at it. I wished I could *really* look after everyone. I'd give Vita a starring part in a TV programme. I'd stop Maxie being so scared of everything and make all the little kids who teased him want him as their best friend. I'd make Dad a Hollywood movie star, though he'd fly back home to us in his own personal jet every weekend. I'd give Mum her own hairdressing salon and she could develop her own range of Julie haircare products.

'Hello?' said Sarah rudely, waving her hand in front of my face.

'Goodbye!' I said.

I dodged past her, caught hold of Vita's hand, and we ran together. Maxie left Dad and clutched my other hand. We all three ran like crazy people, yelling at the tops of our voices.

We ran and ran and ran, along the gravel path and round the pond and right up the hill. I thought Dad would get scared and come rushing after us. I waited for him to start shouting our names.

There were no thudding footsteps, no calls.

When we were almost at the top of the hill Maxie stumbled and fell over again. He lay there, panting. Vita stopped too, clutching her side, her face scarlet. I turned round, the blood drumming so hard in my head there was a red mist in front of my eyes. I blinked. I saw Dad far away below us, a little doll's house father. He had his arms round Sarah. He was kissing her. It wasn't the sort of kiss he gave Mum. It was a real filmstar kiss.

'Yuck!' said Vita.

'Yuck yuck yuck,' said Maxie, sitting up. Then he saw what we were looking at. His bottom lip stuck out. 'Why is Dad kissing that lady?' he said.

I swallowed. 'Because he likes her.'

'Well, we *don't*,' said Vita. 'And now we don't like Dad either. We want to go home.'

'We want to go home,' Maxie echoed.

I wanted to go home too. I hated this cold bleak stupid park.

We walked back down the hill holding hands. They were *still* kissing when we got right down to the bottom.

'He looks like he's eating her, yuck yuck *yuck*,' said Vita. 'Let's creep up on them and give them a big push right into the duckpond.'

We all laughed in a weird high-pitched way.

'Let's do it now,' Vita urged.

I didn't know if she was serious or not. I didn't care. I was suddenly overwhelmed by this image of Dad and Sarah shrieking and splashing. I saw Sarah dripping with green slime, ugly and ridiculous.

'We'll run at them,' I whispered.

But at that moment Dad spotted us. They broke apart. Sarah laughed at our faces. Dad smiled anxiously.

'Hey, you three. Having fun?'

'No, we're not,' said Vita. 'We want to go home.'

'Back to Sarah's?'

'That's not *home*,' said Vita in disgust. '*Our*

home.'

'Not yet, Princess Vita. Come here, darling, let me tell you all about Princess Vita's new holiday home. She has a house right on the top of the cliff made of shells, thousands and thousands of tiny shells stuck in pretty flower patterns—'

'I'm not listening! I don't care about stupid princesses. I'm not listening, not listening, not listening,' Vita chanted, her hands over her ears.

She wasn't a pushover like me. She wouldn't let Dad win her round, though he tried his best. She wouldn't even kiss Dad goodbye when he'd trailed us all the way back home. Dad tried to kiss her anyway. Vita rubbed her cheek fiercely, as if he'd smeared her face with something disgusting. Maxie held his head stiffly to one side so he couldn't be kissed either.

'Oh, kids,' Dad said sadly. He looked at me. 'You'll give me a kiss, won't you, Em?'

I wanted to kiss him, of course I did. I wanted to wind my arms round his neck and beg him to stay. But I kept thinking about the way he'd kissed Sarah. I dodged round Dad and rang our doorbell quickly, ignoring him.

Five

'I can't believe he took you to that woman's flat!' said Gran. 'Here, take those clothes off, Em.'

She pulled them off me so violently it's a wonder my skin didn't come off with them. Mum picked the black jumper up with the tips of her fingers.

'She must be very small, very slim,' she said. 'Is she very pretty, Em?'

'No! Not a bit. She's weird.'

'In what way weird?'

'Like she's got this tattoo on her arm. And her hair's really really short. She looks sort of scruffy,' I said, pulling on my pyjama top.

Vita and Maxie were already in bed, though it had been a struggle to get them there. Vita showed off like anything, prancing around like the dancers in the New Year's Day parade, twirling two old socks above her head like streamers. Maxie got the giggles and then gave himself hiccups and couldn't stop. He kept his mouth open when he hiccuped to sound as grotesque as possible.

I couldn't get them to shut up. Mum didn't even try. She leaned against the bathroom door, staring into space. Gran had to come in and give them a telling-off, scooping them both out of the bath and shaking them hard. She had them dried and dressed in their night things and tucked firmly into bed in ten minutes, with dire warnings if she heard another peep out of them.

She let me stay up because she wanted to know every last detail about Dad and That Woman. Mum started concentrating then, asking me question after question. My head ached trying to tell her the right answers.

'Do you think he really loves her, Em?' Mum asked, her voice a sad little whisper.

Gran sniffed. 'That's not the word I'd use. Frankie doesn't know how to love anyone, not in the real sense of the word.' Gran went off on a rant. Mum and I weren't listening. Mum was looking at me desperately.

I struggled, not knowing what to say. I kept thinking about the way Dad looked at Sarah, the way he followed her around, the way he kissed her. That was love, wasn't it? Then I remembered a word from one of Mum's magazines.

'I think it's just infatuation, Mum.'

Gran laughed and called me a little old woman, but Mum took me totally seriously.

'So you think it's all a five-minute wonder and he'll come back to us?'

'Yes, yes, of course he's going to come back to us,' I said. How could I say anything else?

'You'll be a fool if you take him back,' Gran said.

'OK, I'm a fool. I don't care,' said Mum. 'You don't understand.'

'Too right I don't,' said Gran.

'Haven't you ever been in love, Gran?' I asked.

'You once loved my grandad, didn't you?'

'Look where it got me,' Gran snorted. 'He pushed off and left me stranded with your mum. Still, at least I learned from my mistakes.' She shook her head at Mum.

'You don't always have to be right, Gran,' I said. 'Dad *will* come back, you'll see. It will all come right and we'll be happy again.'

'What's that pink animal flapping past your nose? Whoops, it's a flying pig,' said Gran. 'If you ask me, I doubt you'll ever see him again.'

'We're not asking you. Of course we'll see him. I'll see him every day at the Palace,' said Mum.

The Pink Palace really looks like a palace. It's a huge Victorian building with little towers and turrets. It used to be owned by a big insurance company but they sold it off in the 1960s and someone painted it bright pink all over and turned it into a gift emporium. The pink is faded and peeling now and the towers and turrets are crumbling, but the gift emporium is still there, though half the stalls have closed down.

There are still T-shirt stalls and silver jewellery stalls and second-hand CD stalls and weird stalls that sell all sorts of junk and rubbish. The best stall of all was my dad's Fairyland. It was very tiny, in its own dark little grotto, with luminous silver stars twinkling on the ceiling and a big glitter ball making sparkles all over the floor. There were fairy frocks and fairy wings and magical fairy jewellery, fairy wands and fairy figurines and entire sets of Casper Dream fairy books.

I was the one who gave Dad the idea for Fairyland! When I was much younger I had this embarrassing obsession with fairies. I was desperate to have a proper fairy dress. I can't help squirming now, because I've always been a great fat lump even when I was little, but I still fancied myself in a pink gauze sticking-out skirt with matching wings.

Dad searched everywhere to buy one that would fit me for my birthday. He tried to find a specialist fairy shop. Then he had this brilliant idea. He decided to open his own fairy stall and call it Fairyland.

It was a success at first, because his prices were very low and if kids came along and looked wistful he'd often bung them free fairy bubbles or pixie toffees. He even hired himself out to do themed fairy parties on Saturdays. All the little girls loved him. The mums loved him too. But whenever Dad had an acting job he shut the stall up, and even when he wasn't working he couldn't always be bothered to trail down to the Palace and sit inside his Fairyland. He started to lose customers, so Mum would attach a little card to his white security railings: IF YOU FANCY ANY OF THE FAIRIES, PLEASE APPLY TO JULIE AT THE RAINBOW HAIRDRESSING SALON ON THE THIRD FLOOR.

Mum went into work five days a week, sometimes six when they were short-staffed, and she worked right through till ten on Thursdays, when it was late-night shopping. She really did dye people's hair all colours of the rainbow. Vita and I begged her to dye *our* hair shocking pink or deep purple or bright blue but she just laughed at us.

She went back to work on 2ND January. I stayed at home with Vita and Maxie and Gran. I got out my brand-new journal and sat staring at the first blank page. After ten minutes I wrote: *Saw Dad*. I waited, sucking the end of my pen. Then I closed the journal with a snap. I didn't feel like writing any more.

It was a long long long day. I couldn't wait for Mum to come home. She was later than usual. I started to get excited. Maybe that meant Mum and Dad were having a drink together, talking things over. Maybe right this minute Dad was telling Mum he had made a terrible mistake. Then he'd kiss her the way he'd kissed Sarah. They'd come home together, arms wrapped round each other, our mum and dad.

I went running to the front door as soon as I heard the key in the lock. Mum was standing there all by herself. Her face was grey with the cold and there were snail-trails of mascara down her cheeks.

'It's the wind making my eyes water,' she said, wiping them.

'Did you see Dad?' I asked softly, not wanting Gran to hear.

Mum shook her head. She closed her eyes but the tears still seeped out under her lids. I put my arms round her.

'He'll go to the Palace tomorrow,' I said.

He didn't. He didn't go there the next day or the day after that. He didn't ever have his mobile phone switched on. There was no way we could get hold of him.

'I need his address. Suppose there's some terrible emergency?' said Mum. 'Can't you remember where this Sarah lived, Em? What was the name of the road?'

I thought hard but it was no use. I'd been in such a state of despair and embarrassment I hadn't taken any of it in. I couldn't even remember which station we'd got out at, though Mum made me stare at a tube map to try to jog my memory. I stared until all the coloured lines wavered and blurred. None of the names meant anything to me.

'For God's sake, Em, how could you be so useless?' Mum snapped.

I went off by myself and had a private weep in the toilet. I *felt* useless. I twirled my emerald ring round and round my finger, wishing it was magic so I could conjure Dad from thin air.

I couldn't understand how I'd been so mad with Dad on New Year's Day. Why hadn't I given him a goodbye kiss? I'd have given anything to kiss him now.

I knew Vita felt the same way. She was unusually quiet during the day, sitting curled up with Dancer. She went to bed without a fuss and seemed to go to sleep straight away but when I woke in the night I heard someone sobbing. I thought it was Maxie and stumbled out of bed to his little lair. He was huddled up with his bears, breathing heavily, fast asleep. The sobbing seemed to be coming from my own bed.

'Vita?' I whispered. 'Are you crying?'

She was howling, her head under her pillow. She was wearing Dancer like a big furry glove.

'Hey, come out, you'll suffocate.'

Vita turned away from me, hands over her face, embarrassed.

'It's OK, Vita. Here, have you got any tissues?'

'I've used them all up,' Vita gulped.

'Hang on, I'll go and get you some loo-roll.'

I slipped out of bed again, pulled off a long pink streamer of Andrex and tiptoed back to our bedroom.

'Is that you, Em? Are you all right?' Mum called from her bedroom.

'Yeah, Mum, I'm fine,' I whispered, not wanting to worry her. It sounded like Mum might have been crying too.

I got back into bed with Vita and tried to mop her face for her.

'Get off! I'll do it,' she said fiercely.

When she'd finished wiping and blowing and snuffling I tried putting my arms 'round her. She didn't wriggle away.

'Poor Dancer, you've made her all wet,' I said, feeling her. 'Have you stopped crying now?'

'I'm trying to. But I just keep thinking about Dad and how I wouldn't listen to him and now he's so mad at me he won't come and see me—'

'Rubbish! Dad never gets mad at anyone, especially you, Vita. You know you're his favourite.'

'I'm not!' said Vita, but she sounded hopeful.

'You're *everyone's* favourite,' I said, sighing.

Vita gave a small pleased snort.

'Blow your nose again,' I said, giving her another wad of loo-roll.

She tried to blow her nose with her Dancer hand.

'There now, Princess Vita,' I made Dancer say. 'We all come over a little weepy at times. Let me wipe your little nose for you. There now. Shall I tell you a secret?'

'What?' said Vita.

'You're *my* favourite too. You're much prettier than boring fat old Em and you're not a silly little sausage like Maxie.'

Vita giggled. 'Yes, he *is* a silly little sausage,' she

87

said. She paused. 'Em's a *bit* pretty. She's got lovely hair.'

'She's got a lovely nature too, putting up with a sister like you,' I said.

'When Dad comes next time I'm going to be much much nicer to him,' said Vita, snuffling. 'So long as he doesn't bring that Sarah!'

'She's horrible,' I agreed. 'Dad's gone mad, liking her better than Mum.'

'When I'm married I'm not going to let my husband run off,' said Vita.

'I'm not going to get married at all,' I said. 'It's too easy to pick the wrong person. I'm going to live all by myself and I'm going to eat all my favourite things every day and stay up as late as I like, and I shall read all day and write stories and draw pictures with no one bothering me or fussing or needing to be looked after.'

'Won't you be lonely?' said Vita.

'I shall have a friendly dog and a little cat to curl up on my lap. My sister Vita will come visiting riding on Dancer the Reindeer with her good kind obedient husband and six pretty little girls, and my brother Maxie will come visiting with his big bold wife and his six silly little sausage boys and so I will have more than enough company, thank you.'

'Will Mum come visiting too?'

'Yes, of course. I'll take her on holiday and make her happy.'

'And Dad?'

'He'll come too,' I said. 'He'll have made this fantastic Hollywood movie and be ever so rich and famous so he'll have his own special holiday beach house. We'll all go and stay, and swim and laze on the beach and be happy happy happy.'

'Happy happy happy,' Vita murmured. Then she was still, suddenly asleep.

I lay awake for a long time, trying to tell stories to myself. I could make them seem real enough to comfort Vita, but it was much harder trying to convince myself. I eased Dancer off Vita's hand and made her stroke my head with her furry paws.

'Cheer up, dear old Em,' Dancer said. 'Don't you start crying now. Chin up, big smile, that's my girl. Now, close your eyes and snuggle down and go fast asleep. Fast asleep. Fast fast asleep.'

I didn't manage to go *fast* asleep. It was a very *slow* process, and even then I still woke up very early. I decided to fix myself a bowl of cornflakes and have a private early breakfast with my book. I was rereading *Elsie No-Home* by Jenna Williams. Elsie was good fun, even though she told terrible jokes. I understood exactly how she felt having to look after her little sister and brother all the time.

Mum was sitting at the kitchen table in her nightie, sipping a cup of tea. We both jumped. Mum spilled half her cupful into her black nylon lap.

'I'm sorry, Mum! I didn't mean to startle you,' I said quickly, scared she might get cross with me again.

'It's not your fault, Em,' said Mum. 'Oh come here, love. Don't look so worried. I'm sorry I've been so snappy with you.'

She dabbed at her nightie and then I climbed onto her damp lap. I must have really squashed her but she didn't complain. She held me and rocked me like a little baby.

'My Em,' she said. 'What would I do without you, eh? We've come through thick and thin together, you and me, babe. Do you remember your real dad?'

'A bit,' I said cautiously. I didn't like remembering.

'Whenever he yelled or hit me you'd come and find me crying. You'd put your chubby little arms round me and tell me not to cry, remember? You've always looked after me, Em. And now you look after Vita and Maxie too.'

'So I'm not really useless?'

'Oh don't! I was so mean to say that. I'm sorry, love. Hey, how about coming to the Palace with me today? You be my best girl and help out, yeah?'

I was thrilled at the suggestion. I went off to work with Mum, while Vita and Maxie had to stay at home with Gran.

I loved Violet, the lady who owned the Rainbow Hair Salon. She was quite old, about Gran's age, but she dyed her own hair a crazy pink, and crammed her plump body into very small girly clothes. She always wore hugely high heels, though by the end of the day she usually kicked them off and shuffled round in her stockinged feet.

She pretended not to recognize me. 'So you're the new apprentice, are you, sweetie?' she said. 'How do you do! I'm glad you're coming to work for me. We'd better find you an overall.'

She wrapped a big blue robe round me. It came right down to my ankles but it didn't really matter. I rolled the sleeves up and started cleaning the washbasins and sweeping the floor. When Mum had her first client I rinsed off all the shampoo and wrapped a fresh towel round her neck and then I passed Mum the brush and comb and made the client a cup of coffee while Mum tinted her hair. It was great fun, especially when the client gave me a couple of pounds as a tip! I wasn't sure whether she was joking or not.

I showed the money to Violet, asking if I should put it in the till.

'No, darling, don't be silly! It's all yours. You've jolly well earned it too. You're a nice willing little worker. Your mum can bring you along any time you're off school.'

I grinned at Violet.

'So where's that dad of yours? His fairy shop is still shut up. Can't he get out of bed these days?'

My grin faded. I looked anxiously at Mum.

'Oh, Vi, you know what Frankie's like,' she said lightly.

'Yeah, I know all right,' said Violet, shaking her head. She was looking at Mum intently, her eyes narrowed. She took three pound coins out of the till.

'Here, Em, call these your wages. So now you've got a fiver, right? Why don't you have a little skip round the Palace and see what you want to buy with all this lovely lolly.'

I knew she wanted me out of the way so she could have a proper talk to Mum about Dad. I looked at Mum. She nodded at me. So I sloped off, clutching the five coins in the palm of my hand. I jingled them around, trying to feel pleased I had so much to spend. It was all mine. I didn't have to divide it into three to share with Vita and Maxie. They hadn't earned it, I had.

I went to the T-shirt stall and looked at the five-pound bargain rail. I liked a purple T-shirt with a little cat with diamanté eyes on the front, but it had some funny words on it too.

91

'Maybe your mum and dad might mind. It's a bit rude,' said Manny, the T-shirt guy. He had some very very rude words on *his* T-shirt. 'Maybe your dad could find you a fairy T-shirt,' he suggested.

'Maybe,' I said.

I spent ages at the Fruity Lips make-up booth, trying out all the nail varnish testers, purple, silver and navy blue. My nails were so bitten and stubby I could only fit a slither of colour on each finger. I smeared some sample lipsticks round my mouth and smudged mascara on my lashes experimentally.

'You look beautiful, Em,' said Stevie, the guy who owned Fruity Lips. I think he was maybe kidding me.

'Hey, is Frankie around? I just have to tell him what happened to me over Christmas. I need his advice. It's been the best Christmas ever! Did you guys have a great Christmas?'

'We had lovely presents,' I said carefully.

'Kids!' said Stevie. 'That's all you care about, your presents.'

I didn't argue with him. I wandered down the aisle to the Jewel in the Crown and gently ran my finger along the hanging bead necklaces so that they tinkled. Angelica just laughed. She was always specially friendly to me and let me try on any jewellery I fancied. I tried on every green bangle and bracelet so that they clanked right up to my elbows.

'You're going for the co-ordinated look, right?' said Angelica, flicking her long hair out of her face. She wore so many rings and bangles herself she jangled when she moved.

'Yeah, to match my emerald ring,' I said, showing it to her proudly.

'Oh wow, that's lovely,' said Angelica, holding my hand and admiring my ring from every angle. 'Is it your mum's?'

'No, it's my very own ring. Dad gave it to me for Christmas,' I boasted.

'Your dad is just so wonderful,' said Angelica, sighing. 'His stand is still shut up. Is he coming in today? I was wondering about buying a really big fairy to display some of my jewellery. Do you think he could find one for me?'

'I'm sure he could. I'll tell him when I see him,' I said, and slipped away.

I went right to the end of the aisle. I peered through the white security railings into Dad's darkened Fairyland. The luminous stars stuck on the ceiling shimmered softly. A single strand of fairy lights flicked on and off, on and off, on and off, red and deep blue and amber and glowing emerald green. I looked at the fairies inside, grey and ghostly in the half-light, wings limp, wands trailing.

'Wish for Dad to come back,' I whispered. 'Wish wish wish.'

I shut my eyes and imagined every single fairy waving her wand and wishing, all the big fairy dolls and the little fairy ornaments, all the fairies on the prints and postcards, all the carved fairies on the rosebud soap and the lavender candles, all the pouting baby fairies on the dolls' china tea sets and all the beautiful painted fairies inside all the Casper Dream books.

Six

I was very worried about going back to school. Dad still hadn't come back. I didn't know whether to tell Jenny and Yvonne, my best friends.

We hadn't been friends for that long. I'd only been at this school since we moved in with Gran. It had been horrible trying to fit in with a new class of kids. They didn't treat me like a proper person at first. I was simply Fatty and Greedy-guts and Hippo and The Lump.

Dad heard them calling me names one time last year when he came to collect me from school. He acted like he hadn't heard a thing, but next Monday morning he dropped a handful of tiny silver glittery fairies inside my school bag.

'These aren't selling very well in Fairyland,' he said. 'Maybe you'd like to give a few of your special friends a present?'

He knew I didn't *have* any friends, special or otherwise. The fairies were a cunning bribe. I wasn't sure they would work though. *I* thought the fairies were magical but probably the other girls would think them pathetic or babyish.

I decided I'd keep them incarcerated in my school bag along with my secret comfort Mars bars and Galaxies, but one fell out as I was taking my homework out of my bag and Jenny picked her up.

Jenny was the girl who sat in front of me. She had very glossy neat black hair, bright blue eyes and pink cheeks, just like one of those little wooden Dutch dolls. I'd always liked the look of Jenny. She liked reading and always had a spare storybook stuffed in her school bag. She sometimes read underneath her desk in maths. She wasn't too clever at maths like me, but she didn't seem to care. She wasn't that great at sporty things either. Her cheeks went even pinker when she ran, and her arms and legs stuck out stiffly as if she was really made of wood. She never joined in any games of football or rounders or skipping in the playground. She liked to go over to the brick wall by the bike shed, hitch herself up and sit swinging her legs, reading her book. I always wanted to clamber up beside her and read my book too, but there was one small problem. Yvonne.

She was Jenny's best friend. She really *was* small, only up to Jenny's shoulders, a little skinny girl with a mop of curly red hair. She didn't seem to think much of reading. She didn't sit on the wall beside Jenny, she did handstands up against it, showing us her matchstick legs and her white knickers. She was so-so at most school things but brilliant at arithmetic, so lucky Jenny got to copy off her.

Jenny and Yvonne had very little in common but they'd been best friends since their first day at nursery school together, so it didn't seem remotely possible that they'd ever split up so that *I* could be Jenny's best friend.

They weren't mean to me like some of the other kids. They were so caught up in their own happy best-friend world they barely noticed me. Until Jenny picked up my fairy.

'Oh look! She's so lovely. Where did you *get* her, Emily?' Jenny asked, balancing the fairy on the palm of her hand.

'She comes from Fairyland,' I said.

Jenny looked at me. I blushed scarlet in case she thought I meant a real fairyland.

'It's a stall in the Pink Palace; down near the market,' I said quickly. 'It's called Fairyland. My dad runs it, when he's not acting.'

'Is he that guy with the long hair?' said Yvonne. 'Yeah, I think I've seen him on telly. I saw him in *The Bill* once. So he's your *dad*, Emily?'

'Yes. Well. My stepdad,' I said.

Yvonne rolled her eyes. 'Uh-oh. I've got a stepdad. I can't stick him.'

'Well, my dad's lovely,' I said quickly.

'What a cool thing for your dad to do,' said Jenny, gently throwing the fairy in the air and then catching her. 'Look, she can fly!'

'You can have her if you want,' I said.

'What, just to play with for today?'

'No, to keep.'

'Oh Emily! Really? How wonderful!'

'You lucky thing,' said Yvonne enviously.

'You can have one too,' I said, digging in my school bag.

I didn't particularly want to give a fairy to Yvonne. I liked Jenny much more, but I couldn't really leave Yvonne out.

'Oh wow! Thanks. She can be my lucky mascot,' said Yvonne.

'Em, have you ever read any of Jenna Williams's books?' Jenny asked, floating her fairy through the air.

'Like she's my favourite writer ever,' I said.

'Have you read *At the Stroke of Twelve*? These fairies are just like the ones Lily makes in that book.'

'I know, that's why I like them too,' I said. I thought quickly. 'So, what's your favourite Jenna Williams book, Jenny?'

We had this wonderful long conversation about books while Yvonne sighed a bit and did cartwheels round us and told us were both boring-boring-boring old bookworms. But she was just having a little tease, she wasn't really being nasty. She kept interrupting to ask about my dad and what it was like to be the daughter—well, stepdaughter—of someone famous.

Dad wasn't really *famous*. He'd just had a few small parts on television and appeared in a couple of adverts. He hadn't had his big break yet. Still, I happily showed off about him even so.

I wondered if they'd take any notice of me the next day. I hung back a bit at play time, my heart thumping. I so badly wanted to be friends but I was scared they'd feel I was muscling in. But it was all right! It was more than all right, it was wonderful! Jenna had brought her favourite Jenna Williams book *For Ever Friends* to school with her. I hadn't read it because it wasn't out in paperback yet.

'I thought you might like to borrow it, Emily,' Jenny said. 'Come and sit on the wall with Yvonne and me.'

We were all best friends after that. I knew that Yvonne was still Jenny's best *ever* friend, but I was their second-best friend and that was still great.

They both seemed pleased to see me on the first day of term. Jenny told us all about her Christmas at her auntie's house and how her twelve-year-old cousin Mark had kissed her under the mistletoe and all her family wolf-whistled and Jenny just about died of embarrassment. Yvonne said she'd had *two* Christmases, one on the 25th when she'd stayed at home with her mum and her stepdad and her sisters and they'd had turkey and presents and watched DVDs, and then another on the 26th when she'd gone to her dad and his girlfriend and their new baby and they'd had turkey and presents and watched DVDs. It was the *same* DVD too.

Then they looked at me.

'It started off the best Christmas ever,' I said. 'Dad gave me an emerald ring, a real emerald ring, honest.'

'Oh wow! Your dad's so amazing, like the coolest dad *ever*,' said Yvonne. 'Let's see it then, Em!'

'I'm not allowed to wear it to school of course, but you can maybe come to my house sometime soon and see it. And he bought Vita this wonderful reindeer puppet and Maxie a huge set of felt pens and Mum some silver sandals and Gran some designer jeans.'

'He bought your gran *jeans*?' said Jenny, and started giggling. 'I can't imagine *my* nan in jeans. Still, your gran's ever so slim.'

'I know. It's not fair. So's my mum. I just get fatter and fatter,' I said, pinching my big tummy.

'No, you don't,' Jenny lied kindly. 'You're not really fat, you're just sort of comfortable.'

I wriggled. I didn't feel comfortable. They were my friends. I had to tell them.

101

'But then it all went wrong,' I said. 'There was this row. Then my dad . . .'

I suddenly found tears spurting down my face. I put my head in my hands, scared they'd call me a baby. But Jenny put her arm round me and Yvonne put her arm round me the other side.

'Don't cry, Em,' said Jenny. 'My mum and auntie had a row over visiting my great-grandma in her nursing home, and my dad and my uncle drank too much beer and wouldn't get up to go for a walk on Boxing Day and Mum got mad at Dad. All families have rows at Christmas.'

'Yeah, that's right, Em. My mum found out my dad let one of my sisters have a glass of wine at his house and she just about went bananas,' said Yvonne. 'My mum and dad always have rows at Christmas even though they aren't a family any more.'

'I don't think we're a family either,' I said. 'My dad's got this girlfriend. He walked out to be with her and he hasn't come back.'

I started howling. Jenny pressed closer, her cheek against mine. Yvonne found me a tissue and slipped it into my hand.

'What's up with Fatty?' someone asked, passing by in the playground.

'Don't call Em stupid names,' Jenny said fiercely.

'Yeah, just mind your own business,' said Yvonne.

They bunched up beside me protectively.

'Take no notice, Em,' said Jenny.

'You won't tell anyone?' I wept.

'It's nothing to get worried about. Heaps and heaps of families split up. Your mum and dad still love you, that's what matters,' Yvonne gabbled, like it was a nursery rhyme she'd known since she was little. Then she paused. 'But we won't tell, promise.'

They treated me with extra care and gentleness all day, as if I was an invalid. I got to choose which games we played, I got to share Jenny's lunchbreak banana and Yvonne's box of raisins, I got first go on the classroom computer and the best paintbrush, and when we had to divide up into twos in drama Jenny and Yvonne insisted we had to be a *three*.

They were so kind I found I was almost enjoying myself, though I still had an empty ache in my stomach all the time. It got worse during afternoon school. I started to worry about telling Jenny and Yvonne. It had made it seem too real. Maybe if I'd kept quiet it would all magically come right. *Mum* hadn't told anyone. Violet at the Rainbow Salon had tried her hardest to get her to talk, I knew, but Mum hadn't said a word.

I didn't seem able to keep quiet at all. If I'd only held my tongue when I heard Dad whispering on his mobile to Sarah, then none of this might have happened.

I thought of Dad, Dad, Dad. The ache in my stomach got worse. I hunched up, clutching my front.

'What's the matter, Emily?' said Mrs Marks, our teacher.

'Nothing, Mrs Marks,' I mumbled.

'Well, sit up straight then. And don't look so tragic, dear. I know you find maths difficult, but there's no need to act as if you're being tortured.'

Most of the class laughed at me. Jenny and

Yvonne gave me sad comforting looks, raising their eyebrows at Mrs Marks's attitude. Jenny passed me a hastily scribbled note: *Take no notice of mad old Marks-and-Spencer, you know what she's like. Love J xxx.*

The ache didn't go away though. I kept thinking of Dad looking so sad when I wouldn't kiss him goodbye. I tried to remember that *he'd* done the bad thing by leaving us. He'd inflicted that horrible Sarah on us and she'd made it plain she couldn't stick us. Dad didn't seem to care. If he just wanted to be with her then why *should* we be nice to him?

I knew why. We loved him so.

'I love you, Dad,' I whispered. 'Come back. Please please please come back. I'll do anything if you come back. I'll never ever be mean to you again. I don't care what you've done. I just need to see you. We all need you so. I promise I'll always be good, I'll never ever moan about anything. Please just come *back*.'

The ache got worse and worse. I started to be scared I might throw up in class or have an even more embarrassing accident. I fidgeted around in my seat, praying for the bell to go. When it rang at long last I shot off straight away, not even waiting to say goodbye to Jenny or Yvonne.

I got to the loo in time, thank goodness. I was still ahead of most of the others when I went out into the playground.

I don't know why I looked at the gate. It wasn't as if I was all set to go home. I was ready to go next door to the Infants after-school club. I went there instead of my own Juniors club because I needed to keep an eye on Vita and Maxie. We stayed there till five thirty, when Gran or Mum came to pick us up after work.

I liked helping out with all the little ones, not just my own sister and brother. They all liked me because I told them stories and played with them, all of us squashed up in the Wendy house, and I made them a whole Noah's ark of funny dough animals. I was thinking of making a dough reindeer for Vita to cheer her up. Maybe I could do one for Maxie too. I was working out how to manage clay antlers in my head when I saw the figure standing by the gate. It was a man with a plait.

Seven

'Dad!' I shouted. 'Dad!'

He turned and waved. It really was him. I hadn't made him up. He was there!

I went flying across the playground, through the gate, and then I hurled myself at Dad so hard he staggered and we both nearly toppled over. We clung to each other, swaying and laughing. I dug my fingers into his denim jacket, making quite sure he was real, that I wasn't just imagining him.

'Oh Dad,' I said. 'I was wishing and wishing and wishing you'd come back.'

'And here I am, Princess Emerald. Oh God, I've missed you.'

He gave me another hug. I saw Jenny and Yvonne standing still in the playground, staring dumbfounded at Dad and me, but for once I couldn't be bothered about them.

'I went to pick up Vita and Maxie first but they didn't come out with the other kids. Where are they?'

'They'll be in the after-school club, Dad.'

'Oh, right. Well, let's go and collect them, eh?

I'm taking you kids out for tea. We'll find somewhere really special.'

I wanted to go *home* for tea but I knew that wasn't an option.

'Where are we going then, Dad?'

'Wait for the magical mystery tour, Princess. But I promise your royal highness there'll be chips and candyfloss and ice cream and doughnuts and chocolate—everything you love and you're not normally allowed.'

'Are you kidding me, Dad?'

'I'm deadly serious, sweetheart. Your wish is my command.'

I hung onto his arm proudly, never wanting to let him go. I didn't want to share him with Vita and Maxie. I wanted to keep him just for me for five minutes, but I knew it wasn't fair, so I took him to the after-school club. The moment Maxie saw him he came running across the classroom, scattering crayons and bricks in his wake. Vita hesitated a moment, but then she came running too, bright pink in the face.

'Dad! Dad!'

'Hi, darlings,' said Dad, letting us all hang onto him, giving us a great big hug.

'Well, there's a fine welcome!' said Miss Piper, who runs the after-school club.

'It's cupboard love, because I'm taking them out for a treat tea,' said Dad. 'Come on then, kids.'

We skipped off with Dad without a second thought.

'Your carriage awaits,' he said, leading us to a shiny silver car parked down the road.

We stared, open-mouthed. Our last car had been an old banger that had given up the ghost last year.

110

'You've got a brand-new car, Dad?' I asked shakily.

'You bet,' said Dad, clicking the doors open with his keys. Then he laughed at us. 'Just for today. I've hired it so we can go for a little spin.'

I wasn't sure who Dad meant by 'we'. There was no one waiting in the car, but I wondered if we'd drive straight to Sarah's flat and pick her up too.

'Is it going to be just us?' I said delicately.

'Just us, Princess.'

For one magical moment I wondered if Sarah was already history. Then Dad said, 'Sarah's had to go for an audition. It's such a shame, she really wanted to be in on this little trip. She wants to get to know you all properly.'

We stared at Dad pityingly. Vita rolled her eyes at me. We knew perfectly well Sarah didn't want to get to know us at all. Who did Dad think he was kidding?

'Have you got any auditions lined up, Dad?' I asked, as we set off in the super shiny car. I was allowed to sit in front like a grown-up. I didn't have to cram in the back with Vita and Maxie.

'Oh, I've got all sorts of stuff lined up, Em,' Dad said vaguely.

'It's just I wondered if you had an acting job or an advert or something, seeing as you haven't been at the Palace the last few days,' I said, trying to sound very casual.

'Well, there hasn't been much point. Folk don't hot-foot it to Fairyland at this time of year, right after Christmas. In fact I was wondering about jacking it in altogether.'

'You can't close down Fairyland!' I said.

'Well, maybe that's a bit drastic. I'll think about

it. And meanwhile I'm sure your mum won't mind keeping an eye on it for me.'

'Everyone misses you so at the Palace, Dad. Violet, Manny, Stevie, Angelica . . . and Mum.'

'Well, I miss them all too,' said Dad, staring straight ahead. 'Especially your mum,' he added softly.

'So why won't you come *home*, Dad?' Vita said, leaning forward and poking her face between us in the front.

Dad didn't answer straight away.

'*Dad!*' Vita said sharply, right in his ear.

'Hey, darling, ssh! Now sit back and put your seat belt back on. I've got to concentrate on my driving for a little bit, OK?' said Dad.

'Where are we driving *to*, Dad?' I asked.

'Come on, Em, you're meant to be my bright girl. Where do you get ice cream and chips and candyfloss? We're off to the seaside!'

I stared at Dad. It was a raw dark January afternoon. It didn't seem like a very practical idea. But Dad started talking about paddling and donkey rides and sandcastles so that I almost believed he was talking us to a magic seaside where it was warm and sunny and golden and we'd play on the sands together for endless happy hours. Vita believed it too, and started planning a new bucket and spade and a bag to collect pretty shells. Maxie went very quiet. I worried he might be feeling sick again.

'Are you feeling all right, Maxie?' I asked, craning round.

Maxie ducked his head.

'Dad, we might have to stop, I think Maxie feels sick.'

'Oh God, Maxie, little man, every time I see you

112

now you start projectile vomiting,' said Dad. 'You can't feel carsick, I've only been driving two minutes.'

'I'm *not* feeling sick,' Maxie mumbled.

'So what's bugging you then, Maxie?' I asked.

'I don't want to paddle. The fish will chew my toes,' Maxie said, drawing his feet up onto the car seat and shuddering, as if giant piranha fish were nibbling at him there and then.

Dad roared with laughter. So did Vita.

'Don't laugh!' Maxie said crossly.

'Well, you're so stupid!' said Vita. *'I'm* going paddling, Dad. If I had my costume with me I'd go right in swimming. I'm not afraid of fish, I *like* them. Dad, will you take me to swim with dolphins one day? That would be *so* cool.'

'We'll put that idea on hold for a little while, Princess Vita, but you can paddle with cod and haddock and plaice to your heart's content today.'

We didn't do any paddling though. It was dark by the time we got to the seaside. It was colder than ever, with an icy wind blowing right off the sea.

'Mmm! Breathe in that fresh air,' said Dad, but he was shivering inside his thin jacket.

Maxie's sticking-out ears were painfully crimson, so Dad wrapped my stripy wool scarf round them, tying it in a knot on top of Maxie's head.

'You look like a silly girl with a hair ribbon,' Vita teased. She insisted she wasn't cold but her teeth were chattering, and when I held her hand her fingers were like little icicles.

'Let's run along the sands,' said Dad.

We couldn't find any sand—there were just hard pebbles. We held hands and tried running, making a great crunching din. Maxie kept whining and tripping.

'Ye gods, you're a fusspot, little guy,' said Dad. He picked Maxie up and sat him on his shoulders.

'Pick me up too, Dad!' said Vita.

'Have a heart, darling, I'll keel right over,' said Dad. 'Come on, blow the beach walk. We'll go up on the prom and make for the pier.'

It glittered in the dark, fairy lights outlining the silver domes.

'Is that a palace?' Maxie asked.

'It's the Palace Pier, clever guy. See that stripy tower? That's your very own tower, Prince Maxie, where you can sit on your golden throne and command your magic kingdom.'

Dad bought us food from every single stall on the pier—lemon pancakes and doughnuts oozing jam and salty chips and fluffy candyfloss and 99 ice creams, just as he promised. Vita and Maxie licked and nibbled and slurped until they had food stains all down their school uniform and pink candyfloss scarring their cheeks.

Their hands were too sticky to hold comfortably, so I had to steer them by the shoulders. I ate every scrap of all my takeaways, munching great mouthfuls until my school skirt strained at its zip, but I still didn't feel full enough. The empty ache was there even though I kept telling myself I was having a wonderful day out with Dad and I should be happy happy happy. I'd conjured him up and here he was, all ours.

I started walking very carefully down the pier, trying hard not to step on any cracks whatsoever so that my luck would last and Dad would come back home with us and see Mum and stay for ever. I tried my best, but the pier planks were gnarled and twisted with age and it was hard placing my feet dead centre every single step. I could see through the planks to the dark sea hissing below. It made me dizzy and I had to look up. When I looked down again my shoes were spread all over the place, going over line after line.

Dad saw me looking dismayed. 'What's up, Em? Want another ice cream?'

'Dad, I'm meant to be on a *diet*.'

'Don't you take any notice of your gran. You eat all you want, darling. Come on, let's go in the amusement arcade. I'll see if I can win you all a present.'

There were huge stuffed animals bigger than Maxie decorating the rifle stalls: cream camels with lolling pink tongues; fat elephants with huge flapping ears and tiny twinkly eyes; stripy zebras with stiff black-and-white manes and thick black eyelashes; spotted amber giraffes with long swaying necks and short tufty tails.

Vita and Maxie and I gazed at these luxury animals in awe. Then we looked hopefully at Dad.

'No way, kids. It's all a con. I'd never win enough points,' Dad said.

He tried all the same, changing a ten-pound note into coins, shooting over and over again.

'Tough luck, sir,' the young girl stallholder kept saying, eyeing Dad up and down.

'It *is* tough, darling, when my kids have set their hearts on one of your lovely animals and I haven't got a hope in hell of winning one,' said Dad, giving her his special smile. 'Hey, you've already had one tenner off me. How about I give you another and you make my kids deliriously happy with a camel?'

'I wish I could,' said the girl, sidling up close to

115

Dad and giving him a little smirk. 'But the camels are all counted.'

'An elephant? A zebra? What about that giraffe over in the corner with a wonky neck?'

'My boss would go bananas,' said the girl. 'I can't, I truly can't, not unless you win fair and square.'

'But you know and I know there's no way you can win,' said Dad. 'It's not fair and it's not square.'

'That's life,' said the girl, shrugging. 'Here, your kids can have these as a little consolation prize, eh?' She threw us a packet of jellybeans each.

'Maybe you can come back later . . . without the kids?'

Dad laughed and whispered something in her ear.

Vita glared and tugged at his arm. 'Come *on*, Dad,' she said crossly.

Dad pulled a funny face. 'Sorry, Princess Vita. I'm simply trying to sweet-talk that girl into letting you have a special camel. Still, never mind, let's win you a teddy instead,' he said, stopping at one of those crane machines. Rainbow-coloured teddies were stuffed against the glass, squashed in so tightly their snouts twisted sideways and their beady eyes bulged.

'Uh-oh! They're so crammed in I'll never be able to pull them out,' said Dad.

'But I *want* one,' said Maxie, standing on tiptoe so that he was eye to eye with the huddle of bears.

'You've got hundreds of bears at home, little guy,' said Dad.

'But I haven't got a stripy one. I want *this* one, Mr Stripy,' said Maxie, stabbing the glass with his sticky finger.

116

'I want a bright pink one. It's exactly the colour of Dancer's nose. They can be best friends. Please please please win me the pink one, Dad,' said Vita pleadingly, jumping up and down.

Dad rolled his eyes and then looked at me. 'OK, Princess Emerald, I suppose you want an emerald-green teddy,' he said.

'It's OK, Dad,' I said, though I *did* want one badly. I wanted a very small green bear with bright blue eyes and an anxious expression.

'It's that one, isn't it?' said Dad, pointing to my blue-eyed bear.

'You're magic, Dad,' I said semi-seriously.

'I'll do my best to win you your teddies, but it's not going to be easy,' said Dad.

He changed another ten-pound note and then started manoeuvring the crane. It was the most unwieldy thing ever, the metal claws brushing past each bear uselessly. Sometimes it held onto a paw or an ear or a little snout but after a tug or two it swung away again, empty.

We watched goggle-eyed, holding our breath each time the crane hovered. All four of us went 'Ooooh' at each failure.

On the very last go Dad managed to capture a little lopsided yellow bear that clung onto the crane grimly with one paw.

'Is he mine, Dad?' asked Vita.

'I really wanted Mr Stripy, but the yellow one might do instead,' said Maxie, though he didn't sound sure.

'The yellow ted isn't for you, Maxie. He isn't for you either, little Vita.'

'Is he for *me*, Dad?' I asked.

'Sorry, sweetheart, he's already taken,' said Dad.

117

'He's *mine*.'

'Are you going to call him Mr Yellow?' asked Maxie.

'No, my little bear's called Ray.'

'That isn't a very special name,' said Vita.

'Yes it is, darling. He's my little Ray of Sunshine. He's going to remind me of our happy day together.'

We had one last longing look at Mr Stripy, Pinky and little Blue-Eyes. Then we went out of the amusement arcade, gripping hands and shivering all the way down to the end of the windy pier where the rides were. Maxie cowered away from the dodgem cars and squealed in horror at the great waltzer hurtling round and round.

'You're such a pain, Maxie,' Vita grumbled. 'You're always too scared to go on anything.'

'No I'm not,' Maxie insisted. 'I do want to go on one of the rides. I want to go right up in my tower.'

We looked at the pink-and-red-striped helter-skelter tower.

'I don't think it's *really* got a golden throne inside, Maxie,' I whispered.

'I know,' said Maxie. 'That was just a story, wasn't it, Dad? But it can still be *my* tower, can't it?'

'Of course it's your tower, Maxie. You're very generous and you're happy to share it with Vita and Em and me and all these other people too. But it's going to be dark inside—is that OK?'

'Of course it's OK,' said Maxie bravely.

Dad paid for us all to go into the helter-skelter and climb up and up and up the steps to the top.

'See, Vita, I'm not the slightest bit scared,' said Maxie, his voice just a little squeak.

118

Vita didn't argue. She didn't like it much herself. Halfway up she hung onto my hand and wouldn't let go. When we got to the top at last a man was handing out coconut mats.

'Can I share your golden throne, Maxie?' said Dad, sitting on the mat and pulling Maxie onto his lap.

The man pushed them out onto the slide and they vanished into thin air. We heard Maxie shrieking.

'I don't think I want to,' said Vita. 'Let's go back down the stairs.'

'We can't, Vita, there are people coming up behind us.'

'I don't care.'

'*They* will. Come on. We'll go on a mat together. It'll be OK, you'll see,' I said.

'Aren't you scared, Em?' said Vita.

'No,' I said.

'You're shaking.'

'I'm *cold*. Now come on, get on the mat with me.'

I sat on the mat and Vita perched on my lap, hanging onto my legs tightly with her little pincer fingers. The man gave us a big push and then we were off, out into the dark night, flying round and round and round, the wind in our face and the sea swooshing far below and the lights twinkling all along the promenade. It was as if we'd stepped straight into one of Dad's magic stories. I never ever wanted it to end. It was a shock shooting abruptly right off the slide and landing on the ground, though Dad was there, picking us both up.

'Can we do it again?' we all begged.

Dad gave us another go. This time I took charge

119

of Maxie and Vita flew with Dad. I wished I could have one go on Dad's mat, but Vita was too little to manage Maxie and I knew I was way too big to share with Dad.

I wondered if I should really try sticking to my diet and cutting out all my secret snacks—but when Dad suggested fish and chips for supper I didn't object.

I got frightened when I saw the clock in the fish restaurant. Dad saw me looking.

'Don't worry, Em, it's not twelve o'clock yet. We're not going to turn into pumpkins.'

Vita and Maxie giggled. I waited, eating chip after chip. I ate half of their chips too, trying to get up the courage to ask Dad something.

'You did tell Mum and Gran you were taking us out, didn't you, Dad?'

He shook his head at me. 'You're such an old fusspot, Em. You're my kids. I don't have to ask permission to take you for a fun time.'

I loved it that Dad included me as his kid. But the little worry inside me was getting bigger and bigger.

'But Dad, if you *didn't* tell them won't they be wondering where we are?'

'Just leave it, Em. Don't spoil things,' said Dad.

'Yes, shut up, Em,' said Vita. 'And stop eating my chips. I want to make a little log-cabin house with them.'

'Yes, shut up, shut up, shut up,' Maxie chanted.

Gran always tells us off it we say shut up. Maxie said it over and over again, showing off.

They were both starting to be silly because they were tired out. I was tired too. I felt my eyes pricking with baby tears because Dad had been

120

sharp with me. It wasn't fair. I didn't want to spoil things. But I couldn't help thinking about Mum and Gran and how worried they would be.

'Maybe we could ring Mum?' I mumbled.

'There's no point. We're going to go home now—if that's what you want,' said Dad.

'No, it's *not* what we want,' said Vita. 'We want to stay out with you, Dad. We want to stay out all night.'

'Yes, *all night*,' said Maxie, though his eyes kept drooping and his chin was on a level with his cluttered plate.

I bit my lip. I didn't say any more. Dad paid the bill and picked up Maxie.

'Me too,' Vita wailed, holding her arms up like a toddler.

Dad did his best to carry her as well. I stumped along behind.

'Tell you what, Em,' said Dad, struggling to turn round to me. 'We could all check into a little hotel as the kids are so tired. Then we can drive back tomorrow.'

'But . . . but we haven't got our pyjamas or our washing things,' I said anxiously. 'And we wouldn't be back in time for school tomorrow.'

'Oh, for God's sake, don't be so boring. You sound more middle-aged than your grandmother,' Dad snapped.

I couldn't keep back the tears this time. Dad saw. He stopped. He knelt down with difficulty, Vita and Maxie hanging from either shoulder like rucksacks.

'Em. Em, I'm so sorry. I didn't mean that. I wasn't being serious. I was just playing with the idea. I don't want tonight to end, darling.'

121

'I don't either, Dad,' I sobbed. 'I don't mean to be boring. We can manage without night things—Maxie doesn't even *wear* pyjamas. It would be great to miss school. It's just . . . Mum might think we're never coming back.' I thought of Mum worrying so and I cried harder.

'Don't cry, Em. Please. I can't cuddle you properly with these two. Come nearer, sweetheart. There now. Dry those tears, Princess Emerald. You're the brave little girl who looks after us all and never cries, right? Don't, darling, you're breaking my heart.'

'I've stopped now, Dad,' I sniffed.

'It's OK, baby. I'm going to take you home now. It's going to be all right, Princess Emerald. I'm ordering up your silver carriage right this minute.'

Dad and I settled Vita and Maxie on the back seat.

'Do you want to curl up in the back too, Em? You look exhausted.'

'No, I want to sit with you, Dad.'

I was too anxious to go to sleep. Dad tried telling me elaborate Princess Emerald stories all the way home but I couldn't concentrate properly. He kept losing the thread himself, so that it all started to sound like a dream. We jumped from the princess's palace to her marble swimming pool, but then we were swimming with dolphins way out in the ocean. I started to wonder if it was *all* a dream and I'd wake up all over again on Christmas morning. It would really be the best Christmas ever and Dad wouldn't walk out.

Then we drew up outside our house. The lights were all on. The front door opened and Mum and Gran came running down the front path. They were both crying.

Mum gave me a huge hug and then delved in the back of the car for Vita and Maxie. They were so fast asleep she couldn't wake them up. She started shaking them frantically.

'Vita! Maxie!'

'Hey, hey, they're fine. Don't worry,' Dad said gently.

'Don't *worry*?' said Mum.

She pulled Vita and Maxie out of the car and tried to carry them both, though their weight made her buckle.

'Let me carry them, darling,' said Dad.

'Darling?' said Mum. 'For God's sake, Frankie, stop torturing me. Are you coming back to us now, is that it?'

Dad hesitated. 'Oh, Julie. I still care for you so much. But I've got to be honest. I'm not coming back, my life is with Sarah now.'

Mum's chin shook. She pressed her lips together. Tears slid down her cheeks.

'I wish I could be here. I wish I had the kids around me, I miss them so,' said Dad. 'I love them, Julie.'

'How dare you!' said Gran. She slapped Dad hard across his cheek, her bracelets jangling. 'Do you have any idea how frantic we've been? We thought you'd abducted them. Did you know the police are out looking for you?'

'For God's sake, did you have to bring the police into it? I'm not a kidnapper, I'm their dad.'

'What sort of a dad are you, walking off at Christmas, leaving them desperate, crying their little eyes out.'

'Now come on, I didn't do that, you know I

123

didn't. I tried hard to make it easy for everyone.'

'This is *easy*?' said Mum.

'It's not easy for me either,' said Dad. 'Can't you quit shouting and slapping and making things so horrible and heavy. I wanted today to be lovely for the kids, a treat they'd remember for ever.'

'Why?' said Mum. 'Are you clearing off for good, is that it?'

'Well, Sarah's had this offer with a Scottish theatre. I thought I'd go with her, see if I can maybe get work up there too. But don't worry, babe, I'll come back and see you and the kids as often as I can, even though the fare down is pretty huge.'

'You save your money,' said Gran. 'Though most of it is *my* money that I was fool enough to lend you. We don't want to see you ever again. Push off with your stupid little girlfriend and never ever come back.'

'You don't mean that,' said Dad. He looked at Mum. '*You* don't mean that, do you, Julie?'

'Yes I do,' said Mum. 'Get lost, Frankie. I'm over you already. Let's go for a clean break. I never want to see you ever again, do you hear me? Leave me and my kids *alone*.'

Dad stared at her. One of his cheeks was still scarlet where Gran had slapped him. He rubbed it, looking dazed. Then he took a deep breath.

'OK. If that's the way you want it,' he said. He looked at Vita and Maxie and me. 'What do you want, kids?'

I didn't know what to say, what to do.

I wanted to tell Dad I wanted to see him all the time.

I wanted to tell Mum I didn't ever want to see

124

Dad ever again.

I wanted and wanted, torn in two.

Vita was sobbing now, exhausted.

'What do you want, Princess Vita?' Dad asked softly.

'I want to go to *bed*,' Vita wailed.

Maxie was past saying anything. He was crumpled in a heap in the hallway, whimpering.

'Look at the state you've got them in,' said Mum. 'What sort of a dad are you?'

'OK, OK. I'm a lousy dad, a useless husband, a hopeless provider,' Dad shouted. 'Right then, I'll make everybody happy. I'll clear off out of your lives. We'll go for a clean break.'

He jumped back in his silver car, started the engine and zoomed off into the night.

Eight

Dad didn't come back. It looked as if he meant it.

A clean break.

He sent Mum a cheque with a Scottish postmark on the envelope. He didn't put his address. He didn't write a letter either. He just scribbled on the back of the cheque, *Love from Frankie and xxx to the kids*.

'That's not a proper letter we can keep,' I said sadly.

'It's not a proper cheque either,' Gran sneered. 'He still owes me thousands and yet he's acting like Lord Bountiful sending your mum a cheque for a hundred pounds. As if that's proper maintenance!'

A hundred pounds seemed a huge amount to me. I thought of running round the Flowerfields shopping centre with a hundred gold coins in my school bag. I could go to the Bear Factory and buy a cuddly black cat with his own cute pyjamas; go to the bookshop and buy an entire set of Jenna Williams stories; go to Claire's Accessories and buy all sorts of slides and scrunchies and glittery make-up; go to the Pick 'n' Mix Sweetstore and choose a whole sackful of sweets . . . and I'd *still* have heaps left to buy presents for Vita and Maxie.

Then I thought of all the boring stuff like bills in brown envelopes and cornflakes and loo-rolls and spaghetti and milk and Maxie's new school shoes and Vita's leotard for ballet and my new winter coat. Maybe a hundred pounds wasn't very much after all.

I put Dancer on my hand and made her talk to me.

'Cheer up, Princess Emerald,' she said. 'Your dad won't let you down. He's the most wonderful man in the world, you know he is. I'm sure he'll send another cheque soon. This time there'll be a proper letter you can keep, just you wait and see.'

I waited. Dad didn't send anything. He didn't pay his rent to the Pink Palace either. The fairies grew dusty behind their bars.

'I don't know what to do,' Mum said. 'I can't keep it on. I can't be in two places at once. It never brought in much money even when Frankie was around. We'll have to let it go.'

'You can't let them close Fairyland!' I said, appalled. 'What will Dad do when he comes back?'

'Get this into your head once and for all, Em. He's not coming back,' said Mum, taking hold of me by the shoulders and speaking to me practically nose to nose.

'Yes he is, yes he is, yes he is!' I said inside my head.

I made Dancer whisper it to Vita and Maxie and me every night when we went to bed. We all believed her. Maybe Mum did too, in spite of what she said. She paid the Fairyland rent herself right up until Easter.

130

We'd all started hoping that Dad would come back then, even if it was just for a visit. He always made such a special day of Easter. I remembered one Easter, when Vita was very little and Maxie was just a baby, Dad hired a huge rabbit costume from a fancy dress store and pretended to be the Easter Bunny, crouching down and hopping, flicking his floppy ears from side to side.

Another year he hid hundreds of tiny wrapped chocolate eggs in every room of the house and all over the garden, and we spent all Easter morning running round like crazy, seeing who could find the most (me!).

Last year Dad gave us all different eggs. Maxie got a big chocolate egg wrapped in yellow cellophane with a toy mother hen and three fluffy chicks tucked into the ribbon fastening. Vita got a pink Angelina Ballerina egg with a tiny storybook attached. I got a Casper Dream fairy egg with a set of Casper Dream flower fairy postcards. He gave Mum a special agate egg, with whirls of green and grey and pink, very smooth and cool to touch.

'It's called a peace egg,' Dad told her. 'You hold it in your hand and it calms you down when you're feeling stressed.'

Mum held her agate egg a lot through January and February and March. Sometimes she rolled it over her forehead as if she was trying to soothe all the worries inside her head. She held onto it most of this new Easter Day.

Mum tried her hardest to make it a special day. She made us our favourite boiled eggs for breakfast and she even drew smiley faces on each one.

We had chocolate eggs too, big luxury eggs with bright satin ribbons. When we bit into them, teeth clunking against the hard chocolate, we found little wrapped truffles inside. Mum said we could eat as much chocolate as we wanted just this once—but we were all keyed up waiting for Dad to come with *his* Easter surprises.

We waited all morning. Gran cooked a chicken for lunch. We waited all afternoon. Gran suggested we all went for a walk in the park but we stared at her as if she was mad. We didn't want to risk missing Dad.

'He's not going to come,' Gran said to Mum. 'You *know* he's not. You haven't seen sight or sound of him since that dreadful day when he ran off with the kids.'

'He didn't run off with us, Gran. It was just a day out,' I said heavily.

'A day and half the night, with the police out searching,' Gran sniffed.

'I *have* heard from him,' Mum said. 'You know he sent another cheque last week. And he put *Happy Easter* to all of us. So I thought . . .' Mum's hand tightened on her peace egg.

'You thought he'd come running back with his silly fancy presents, getting the kids all over-excited and driving you mental,' Gran said.

'Shut *up!*' Mum shouted. She suddenly flexed her arm and hurled her peace egg to the other side of the room. It landed with such a clunk we all jumped. The peace egg stayed smoothly intact, but it dented Gran's video recorder and chipped a big lump out of Gran's skirting board.

'Oh God, I'm sorry!' Mum said, starting to sob.

We thought Gran would be furious. Her eyes filled with tears too. She went to Mum and put her arms round her.

132

'You poor silly girl,' Gran said. 'I can't bear to see you sitting all tense and desperate, longing for him. You're making yourself ill. Look how thin you've got.'

I looked at Mum properly. I hadn't noticed. She really had got thin. Her eyes were too big in her bony face, her wrists looked as if they would snap, and her jeans were really baggy on her now, so that she had to keep them up with a tight belt.

It wasn't fair. I missed Dad every bit as much as Mum and yet I hadn't got thin, I'd got fatter and fatter and fatter.

It didn't stop me creeping away and eating my entire Easter egg all in one go. I licked and nibbled and gnawed until every last crumb was gone. My mouth was a mush of chocolate, pink tongue covered, my teeth milky brown. I imagined my chocolate throat and chocolate stomach. Yet I *still* felt empty. I was like an enormous hollow chocolate girl. If anyone held me too hard I'd shatter into a thousand chocolate shards.

I felt so lonely during the Easter holidays. Whenever we went out to the shops or the park or the swimming baths there were fathers everywhere. They were making the teddies talk to the little kids in the Bear Factory; they were helping them feed the ducks and pushing swings and kicking footballs; they were jumping up and down playing Ring-a-Ring o' Roses in the water.

There were dads in every television programme, making a fuss of their kids. One time we even spotted *our* dad in an old film. It was just a glimpse, in a crowd, but the plait was easy to spot.

'It's Dad, it's Dad!' I said.

'*Dad!*' Vita screamed, as if he could hear her.

133

Maxie didn't say anything. He turned his back to the television. He'd stopped talking about Dad the last few weeks. He just looked blank when Vita and I said his name.

'Maybe he's forgotten him,' said Vita, when we were getting ready for bed. Gran was in the bathroom with Maxie, washing his hair. He'd poured concentrated Ribena over his head because he said he wanted to dye his hair purple.

'Don't be silly, Vita, he can't possibly have forgotten Dad already.'

'Well, he's such a baby. And totally weird,' said Vita.

'I know, but it's only three months since we saw Dad.'

'Three months two weeks and four days,' said Vita.

I stared at her. Vita could barely add two and two.

'How do you know so exactly?'

'Because I've been marking it off on my calendar,' said Vita.

'What calendar?'

'I made it at school just before Christmas. We had to stick it on an old card and do glitter and I got bored and did a red-glitter bikini on Jesus' mummy and my teacher got cross with me and said I'd spoiled my calendar and couldn't send it to anyone. So I put it in my desk and now I mark off the days,' said Vita.

'You could have given the calendar to Mum or Dad. Dad would have found it ever so funny,' I said.

'Well, I could give it to him when he comes back. I could do red-glitter hearts all round the edge of the dates,' said Vita.

I thought of her own little red heart thumping with love for Dad underneath the fluffy kitten jumper Gran had knitted for her. I didn't always *like* Vita but I loved her a lot. I wanted to give her a big hug but I knew she'd wriggle and fuss and say I was squashing her. I put Dancer on instead and she gently hugged Vita's little stalk neck and blew breathy kisses into her ear.

'Make Dancer kiss *me*,' Maxie said, running into our room stark naked. His newly washed hair stuck up in black spikes.

'Dancer doesn't want to kiss silly little bare baby boys,' said Vita primly. 'Put something on, Maxie. We don't want to see your woggly bits. I'm so so glad I'm a girl, aren't you, Em? Dad always said I was his favourite little girl.'

'He said I was his favourite grown-up girl,' I said.

I wondered if he said that to Sarah now.

Maxie didn't join in. He gathered up all his bears, a great tatty furry bundle. 'We're all bears,' he shouted. 'I'm bare and they're bear! We're all bears.' He shrieked with laughter and yelled it over and over again, in case we hadn't got it the first time. We did our best to ignore him, so he started nudging us with his teddies. He got wilder, bludgeoning us with bear limbs. One paw went right in my eye and hurt a lot. I *frequently* didn't like Maxie and recently it was very hard to remember that I loved him.

He'd always been silly but now he acted positively demented, running around all over the place, yelling his head off, throwing baby tantrums in the supermarket and the street. Mum worried he might have some serious problem and thought she should take him to the doctor.

'That child doesn't need a doctor, he needs an old-fashioned smack bottom,' said Gran. 'Plus a daily dose of syrup of figs to keep him regular. He spends hours in that toilet! Still, I'm not surprised—all his finicky ways with his food: won't eat this, won't eat that, and fuss fuss fuss if his beans touch his egg or his chips aren't in straight lines, for pity's sake. I'd never have let you play me up like that, Julie.'

'Maxie's traumatized, Mum,' our mum protested.

'Nonsense, he's simply spoiled rotten. I've always thought you were an idiot pandering to him the way you do, giving in to every little fear and fancy. You've got to help him toughen up. After all, Maxie's going to have to be the man of the family now.'

Vita and I collapsed into helpless laughter at the idea of Maxie the Man protecting us in any way whatsoever. Mum was near tears but she started snorting with laughter. Even Gran couldn't help smiling. Maxie himself ran amok, laughing like a hyena though he didn't understand the joke.

We called him Maxie the Man after that. For a couple of days he strutted around, growling in as deep a voice as he could manage, calling Vita and me his 'little girlies'. He did his best to boss us about. We put up with it for a while because it was quite funny at times. Mum and Gran joined in, letting Maxie order them around. He took to calling Mum 'Woman!' and it always made her laugh.

'Don't you go calling *me* Woman, you saucebox,' said Gran, shaking her finger at Maxie.

136

'Gran's *Old* Woman!' I whispered to Vita.

'I heard that!' Gran said sharply. 'I don't think we should encourage Maxie. He'll carry on in the same manner when he's back at school, trying to tell all the teachers what to do.'

Gran had a point. I tried to get this across to Maxie but he just stood shaking his head at me, hands on his funny little hips.

'Don't take that tone of voice with me, Little Girlie,' he said, coming out with one of Gran's favourite phrases. 'Kindly remember, I'm the Man of the House.'

'No, you're not, you silly little squirt,' said Vita irritably. '*Dad's* the Man of the House.'

Maxie didn't react.

'Maxie, you do remember Dad, don't you?' I asked.

Maxie shrugged. He tried to tell us off again, his hands clutching his sides so tightly that his shorts rose comically up each leg.

'You look so stupid,' said Vita. 'No wonder they call you names at school.'

'What names do they call him?' I asked. They called *me* names and it was horrible. I couldn't stand it if little Maxie was being teased like that too.

'They call him *heaps* of different names,' said Vita.

'No they don't!' said Maxie.

'Yes they do. All the Infants call him stuff.'

'Like *what*?'

'Maxie wee-wee, Maxie pee-pee, Maxie widdle—Oooh!'

Maxie leaped up at Vita and yanked her wispy hair so hard he pulled out a whole hank. Vita

137

shoved Maxie violently. He toppled and banged his head, hard. Vita jumped on top of him and banged his head again, harder.

Mum and Gran came rushing. They had to prise them apart, both scarlet and screaming.

'For pity's sake, what's the matter with you both? Are you trying to kill each other?' said Gran, shaking them.

'Yes!' they both roared.

'Come on, I'm not having children behaving like little devils in my house. Up to bed this minute, both of you.' Gran seized hold of them by the wrists and started hauling them upstairs.

'Mum, stop it, they're *upset*,' said our mum. 'Leave them be. Come on, Maxie, Vita, stop crying. Come and I'll read you both a story.'

Gran shook her head. 'That's plain silly, rewarding them for temper tantrums.' She glared at me. 'Why are you standing there so gormlessly, Em? Can't you keep your little brother and sister out of mischief for two minutes?'

This was so horribly unfair I couldn't bear it.

'Why should I always have to sort them out just because I'm the eldest? I'm not their mother!' I said.

'Now stop that! You should be glad to help out. Your own mum is doing her best but she can't cope.'

'I *can* cope! You mind your own business, Mum!' our mum shouted. 'I know you mean well but I'm sick of you bossing the kids around and being so strict with them all the time. They're not being deliberately naughty. They're *unhappy*. We're all bloody miserable.'

'For pity's sake, I'm only trying to help,' said

Gran. 'It's time you got a grip. It's been months since that idiot walked out. Can't you get over him?'

'No I can't,' said Mum. 'Come on, kids. We'll go upstairs and leave Gran in peace.'

'Are we still being sent to bed?' said Vita, as we went upstairs.

'Well, how about if we all come and cuddle up in my bed?' said Mum.

'Just Vita and Maxie?' I said.

'No, no, you too, Em darling. All of us. We'll read stories and play games and I've got some chocolate tucked away somewhere.'

We all got into our night things and crammed in Mum's bed, though it wasn't as much of a squash now. Vita stroked Dad's pillow.

'Is it lonely not having Dad to cuddle up with?' she said.

'Of course it's lonely, Vita,' I said. I still often heard Mum crying if I had to get up in the night to go to the loo.

'Yes, it's very lonely,' Mum said. 'I sometimes take Dad's pillow and tuck it in beside me and then in the middle of the night when I'm asleep it's as if he's there.'

'You can borrow Dancer sometimes if you like,' said Vita, making Dancer stroke Mum with her velvety paw.

'You can have one of my teddies,' said Maxie, patting Mum too.

Mum started talking more about Dad, telling us all the things she really missed, the way he hummed under his breath, the way he always invented some new sweet pet-name for her, the way he hugged her, the feel of his lovely long dark plait . . .

139

Vita and I started crying, remembering too. Maxie stayed dry-eyed, his pats changing to sharp little slaps.

'Shut up, Mum,' he said. 'Shut up, shut up, shut up.'

'Now then, Maxie, you know you're not supposed to say shut up. And I don't *want* to shut up. I want to talk about Dad and how sad I am. I want you three to talk about him too. It might help us feel a bit better if we talk about him.'

'Maxie's forgotten Dad,' Vita snuffled.

'Don't be silly, sweetheart, of course he hasn't,' said Mum.

'He *has*. Maxie, who's Dad?' said Vita.

'Don't know, don't know, shut up, shut up,' said Maxie, struggling out from under the covers.

'Ssh now, Maxie. Snuggle back in, darling,' said Mum. 'Oh dear, I know you don't want to talk about Dad and yet I think we should.'

'He's coming back soon, Mum, we know he is,' said Vita.

'Well, we *wish* he'd come back,' said Mum.

'Em wished it. It will come true,' said Vita. 'We just mustn't ever give up. That's right, isn't it, Em? Dancer says so.'

I took Dancer and made her nod her head.

'I'm magic, my dears. I've lived with Santa and he's taught me all his little tricks. He frequently confided in me. I was his right-hand reindeer.' I made Dancer wave her right paw in the air, showing off.

They all laughed. I did too. It was so weird. I was working Dancer, making it all up as I went along, and yet it was almost as if she was a real separate person saying things I'd never think of.

140

She told us a long story about a child who asked for her dad to come back as her Christmas present. Santa had to search for this dad all the way across the world to Australia. It was stiflingly hot and sunny so Santa went as red as his robes and the furry reindeer were all exhausted, so they cooled off on Bondi beach. Santa paddled with his robes tucked up round his waist, showing his baggy longjohn pants. Dancer and all the other reindeers swam in the surf, seaweed swinging from their antlers. Then they all renewed their search and found the dad shearing sheep. It turned out he was on such a remote farm there wasn't a postbox, so he didn't know how much his daughter was missing him. As soon as he realized he jumped onto the sleigh with Santa, and Dancer and the team of reindeers galloped all the way across the world. The dad jumped off the sleigh at dawn and went running into the house. He woke up his little daughter—

'And she cried, *Daddy, oh my daddy*,' said Vita. She frowned. 'But if Santa was dashing off to Australia and back how could he deliver all the children's presents too?'

'I don't know,' I said, irritated. 'He can manage anything. He's magic, like I said.'

'I think your story was magic, Em,' said Mum. 'You're so good at making up stories. You obviously take after Dad. He could always make up wonderful things.'

'She can't take after Dad,' said Vita. 'He's not Em's real dad. He's *my* dad.'

'He's been a lovely dad to Em too,' said Mum. 'I think he's helped her make up super stories. You should write them down, Em. I'd love to keep

141

them.'

'To show Dad when he comes back?'

Mum sighed. 'Darling, we've got to start thinking he's not coming back.'

'He is coming back, Mum. He is, he is, he is,' I said.

'Oh, Em. Do you really think if we say it enough times it will come true?' said Mum.

'It will,' I said.

'Definitely,' said Vita. 'Yes yes yes.'

'Yep,' Maxie mumbled, but he was half asleep.

*   *   *

The next day Mum sidled up to me when she came home from work.

'Here, Em, I've got you a little present. Don't let on to Vita and Maxie or they'll feel hard done by.' She handed me a paper bag. There was a familiar rectangular shape inside.

'Oh Mum, is it the new Jenna Williams book?'

'You and that Jenna Williams! No, take a look.'

I took a shiny red book out of the bag. I tried not to feel disappointed. I opened it up and saw blank pages.

'It's for your Dancer stories.'

'Oh.' I wasn't sure this was such a good idea. It was so much easier just *telling* them. If I wrote them down I'd have to plan it all out and remember all the boring stuff about punctuation and paragraphs. And never beginning a sentence with 'And'.

Mum was looking at me anxiously.

'Great,' I said, sounding false. 'Thank you very much.'

'You don't *have* to write the stories,' said Mum. 'I just thought it might take your mind off things. But it's not meant to be hard work, it's meant to be fun.'

'Do I have to do it like at school?'

'No, you write it however you want,' said Mum. 'Draw pictures too, if you like.'

I started to get more enthusiastic. I decided I'd do lots of pictures. I'd colour them in. I'd *maybe* use a certain nearly new set of beautiful felt-tip pens.

Maxie never seemed to use them nowadays. He'd done a handful of his wonky doughnut people during the Christmas holidays, but then he scribbled over all of them with the black pen.

Gran said she'd take them away from him if he just did silly scribbling, though she said it wasn't Maxie's fault, he was far too young to own such an expensive set of pens.

Mum said Gran didn't have the right to take them away from Maxie, though she did privately beg Maxie to use them properly. She'd found a lot of black scribble on the wall beside Maxie's mattress and had spent ages scrubbing with Vim.

Maxie didn't use his pens at all after that, though he guarded the big tin carefully and shrieked if Vita or I went near them.

I waited until he was fast asleep in his bear lair and Vita was snuggled up with Dancer. Then I crept out of bed, tiptoed across the carpet and very cautiously felt under Maxie's mattress. I found the great big smooth tin of felt tips and gently eased them out, careful not to make them rattle. I took them to the bathroom with me. I put all the towels bunched up in the bath to cushion it and then hopped in with my new notebook and Maxie's pens.

I opened the red notebook up and smoothed out the first page. I selected the black pen, ready to write 'Dancer the Reindeer' in my best swirly handwriting. The black came out as a faint grey trickle. It was all used up.

Maxie had obviously been doing a lot of secret scribbling somewhere or other. It looked like Mum was going to have to buy another can of scouring powder.

I chose the scarlet pen instead. It came out the palest pink. Maxie had used the red up too! I tried the gold, the purple, the brightest blue. They were nearly all completely used up. The only pens still working were Maxie's least favourite colours, the dark greens and all the browns.

I couldn't understand it. I'd not seen Maxie using them. How could they possibly all be used up already?

I had to start my Dancer story using my own inferior gel pens. I didn't know how to get started properly. It sounded so silly and babyish writing Dancer the Reindeer did this, did that. It was so much more interesting when she told her own story.

I had a sudden idea. I crept back to the bedroom, eased Dancer out from under Vita, and went back to my special bath. I put Dancer on my right hand and tucked a pen between her paws.

'What's this?' she said, twiddling it around.

'You know what it is. It's my special pink gel pen, to match your pretty pink nose. I want you to write your story for me, Dancer. Tell it like an autobiography, right from the beginning, when you

144

were born.'

'When I was a tiny fawn, all big eyes and no antlers?' said Dancer.

She breathed in deeply, wriggled the pen more comfortably in her paws, and began.

I am Dancer, a reindeer. I was born in a blizzard, such a deeply snowy night that my poor mother could not find shelter for us. She did her best, arching her poor weary body over me, while I nuzzled up to her weakly, up to my snout in thick snow. You would think this chilly start in life would leave me susceptible to colds, but although I am of dainty build even now in my middle years I have always prided myself on my stout constitution. I never have a cold or a chill or any bout of flu. My nose stays prettily pink, never ever red and shiny. I would feel I was seriously blemished if I was famous for being a red-nosed reindeer, and had a popular song written about me.

I do not wish to boast but I am sure I am equally famous for my dancing skills. I can do ballroom, I can bop like a demon, I can tap up a storm, but my speciality is ballet. I am the Anna Pavlova of the reindeer kingdom.

I pressed Dancer's pink nose and made the 'Sugar Plum Fairy' music tinkle. Dancer twirled round and round, her net skirt whirling. She pirouetted up and down the bath and then jumped on and off the taps.

'I'm doing my tap dance now!' she announced.

We both hooted with laughter.

'Em?' Mum knocked at the bathroom door.

145

'Em, what are you up to in there? What are you doing out of bed? Who's in there with you?'

'Just Dancer, Mum,' I said. I clambered out of the bath and let her in.

'You and Dancer! You're a daft girl,' said Mum. 'I can't get over the way you kids act like she's real. You're daft as a brush, babe. Still, you're good at making up her stories. Have you started writing them in your new book?'

'Yep!' I said, flashing a page at her.

'You've been writing in the *bath*?' said Mum, looking at the scrunched-up towels.

'It's my special writing couch, Mum,' I said.

'For goodness' sake,' she said. 'You're not meant to be writing now. You're meant to be fast asleep in bed.'

'Haven't you heard of burning the midnight oil, Mum? I'm inspired!'

'You've got an answer for everything, my Em,' said Mum, giving me a hug. 'Let's read your story then.'

'Not yet. Not till it's all finished and I've filled the book right up.'

'There, it was a good idea of mine, wasn't it? I got blank pages instead of lined so you can do as many pictures as you like. Maybe Maxie will let you borrow his fancy felt tips if you ask him really nicely.'

'Maybe,' I said.

I decided not to tell on Maxie. I needed to do my own investigating first.

*   *   *

I didn't tackle him directly. I simply kept an eye on

146

him the next day. I watched him sneak the dark brown pen out of his tin and stick it down his sock when he was getting dressed.

I followed him round doggedly, though it was very tiring. Maxie dashed here, charged there, darted up and down the stairs, running riot everywhere. He jumped on Mum, he badgered Gran, he tugged my hair, he pinched Vita. He knocked the cornflakes packet over, he spilled his juice down his front, he tripped over the vacuum and screamed blue murder—but he *didn't* take the felt pen out of his sock to scribble.

I waited patiently, biding my time. Maxie went to the loo. I followed him upstairs to the bathroom and waited outside. I waited and waited and waited. Gran was right, Maxie had started to take an awfully long time in the loo.

I was needing to go myself. I got fed up waiting. I knocked on the door. 'Maxie? Come on out, you must be finished now.'

'Go away, Em,' Maxie said, the other side of the door.

'Maxie, you've been in there fifteen minutes. What's the matter? Have you got a tummy upset?'

'No! Just bog off!' Maxie yelled crossly.

He knew he wasn't meant to say this. It was an expression he'd picked up off a television programme and it drove Gran nuts.

'I'm not bogging off anywhere, Maxie. You come *out*!' I paused. 'I know what you're up to in there!' I hissed through the keyhole.

'No you don't!' said Maxie, but he sounded panicky.

'You come out or I'll tell,' I threatened.

Maxie went quiet. Then he suddenly unlocked

the bathroom door and came out.

'You're not allowed to lock yourself in, you know that,' I said. 'What if you get stuck?'

'I'd jump out the window,' said Maxie. 'Like this.' He jumped along the hallway like a giant frog. He was jumping slightly awkwardly, his hands clamped over his T-shirt chest. I knew that problem. He was hiding something.

I played along with him, jumping too, pretending to be a fellow frog. Maxie croaked delightedly, wobbled, and threw out his arms. It was my chance. I slid my hand up his T-shirt and grabbed. I came away with a giant wad of crumpled pink loo-roll.

'Yuck!' I said, dropping it immediately.

'Don't, don't, don't!' Maxie screamed, though I'd already done it.

'Maxie, what are you playing at? You throw the used loo-roll down the toilet, you don't stick it up your T-shirt!' I said. I caught hold of his wrists as he scrabbled to get hold if it.

'Give it me back!' Maxie roared.

'No, it's dirty!' I cried.

But when I looked properly I saw it hadn't been used in the way that I'd feared. There were at least twenty separate sheets of loo-roll. Each one had been scribbled over with Maxie's brown felt pen. Not any old angry silly scribble. This was a very careful painstaking up and down long string of nearly-letters, all the way down to the bottom of each strip. Then there was a wobbly M for Maxie and a whole line of uneven xxxx.

'These are letters, Maxie,' I said. I let him go and started smoothing them out.

'Give them *back*,' said Maxie, hitting me.

'Who are these letters to, Maxie?' I asked,

although of course I knew.

'Shut *up*, Em!' Maxie wailed.

'Emily, what are you doing to your little brother?' Gran called from downstairs.

'Nothing, Gran. I'm just sticking his head down the loo and using it like a toilet brush,' I called.

'You're doing *what*?' Gran shrieked.

'Joke, Gran, just *joking*,' I said. 'I'm just sorting Maxie out, that's all.'

Then I knelt in front of Maxie on the landing, my nose nearly touching his. 'They're letters to Dad, aren't they, Maxie? You haven't forgotten him one little bit. You just don't want to talk about him because it hurts, right?'

'No no no,' said Maxie, but big fat tears were starting to spurt down his cheeks.

'What are you saying in your letters? Are you asking him to come back?'

'I'm saying I'll be a big brave boy if he comes back,' Maxie wept.

'Dad doesn't mind you being little and silly,' I said. I gave him a big hug. He struggled for a bit but then relaxed against me, rubbing his thatch of black hair into my neck.

'I've written him millions and millions of letters,' he said.

'But what did you do with them all?'

'I posted them. Properly, in the postbox down the shops. Gran wasn't looking,' Maxie said proudly.

I thought of all those tattered loo-roll letters clogging up the bottom of the postbox.

I nearly cried too.

Nine

When we went back to school we had to learn how to wire up a circuit in technology.

'That's good,' said Gran. 'My entire house needs rewiring and I haven't got the money to get it sorted. Maybe you'll do it for us, Em.'

She didn't really mean it. She was being sarcastic.

Mrs Marks, our teacher, suggested we use a clown's face with a dicky bow tie and a nose that could light up if we wired the circuit properly.

'Don't let's do a boring old clown,' I begged Jenny and Yvonne. 'Let's do Dancer, and have a pink light for her nose!'

'You're obsessed by that flipping reindeer,' said Yvonne, who'd heard one too many Dancer stories.

In our art lesson I painted a portrait of Dancer in the style of Picasso, with her antlers lopsided, her legs all over the place and both her eyes on one side of her head. I thought it was a very good painting. I gave it to Vita as a present but she wrinkled her nose at it.

'Dancer doesn't look a *bit* like that,' she said.

'Even Maxie knows where the eyes go on your head, one either side of the nose.'

'Well, you can stick Dancer's antlers right up *your* nose,' I said crossly.

In drama we had to act out the Seven Deadly Sins. I chose Wrath. I got very angry indeed. I had Jenny and Yvonne as my partners and they got quite scared when I screamed at them.

'I was just *acting*,' I said.

'Well, you're a bit too good at it,' said Jenny.

I wasn't good at maths at all, I was totally hopeless. We were learning about percentages and I was 100 per cent hopeless at it. Mum found me rubbing out frantically on Sunday night, unable to get the right answer to anything.

'Can't you tell the teacher you don't understand how to do them?' said Mum. She peered at my messy figures. '*I* don't have a clue. Can the other children do it? What about Jenny and Yvonne?'

'Yvonne's brilliant at maths. Jenny sits right next to her and she can copy off her. Then when we have homework Jenny gets her dad to do it.'

Mum sighed. 'Well, even if your dad was home here, he couldn't do any sums to save his life. You could try asking your gran.'

I decided I'd sooner get into trouble at school. Gran was in a really mean crabby mood a lot of the time now.

'I know she's a bit cross, Em. She's tired having to work so hard. She's paying all the bills now and she's fed up about it,' Mum whispered.

I knew money was a Big Problem. Dad hadn't sent any more cheques at all, and Mum wasn't making much money at the Rainbow Hair Salon.

'Gran thinks I should report Dad and get the

154

courts to make him send child support regularly,' said Mum. 'I know I maybe *should*, but it seems so awful. And if he hasn't been able to get work in Scotland then he won't have any money anyway. I'm sure he'd send something if he could.'

We were learning about the Tudors in history. Henry VIII made Dad seem like a very *good* husband. I hated it when Gran went on and on about him. I was sorry her work made her tired, but at least she was just sitting in an office, not on her feet all day like Mum. We were learning about an Indian village in geography where old ladies like Gran had to trek backwards and forwards with great sticks or big water pots on their heads, and toil all day in the fields.

I had to do an awful lot of toiling at school in PE because we were practising for our sports day. It was all right for Yvonne. She came first every time we raced, she jumped the highest and the longest, she leaped the furthest in the sack race, she won the egg and spoon race *without* cheating with Blu-tack. She even won the three-legged race tied up to Jenny. Yvonne would have won a *no*-legged race.

At least Jenny was almost as slow as me when we practised. We huffed and puffed at the very end of each race. I think Jenny might have been able to run a little bit faster but she was kind enough to slow down and keep me company, so we were equal last. As Jenny and Yvonne were partners in the three-legged race Jenny suggested she and I join up for the wheelbarrow race.

We didn't do *too* terribly when I was the runner and Jenny was the wheelbarrow, but after a few minutes Mrs Marks blew her whistle and said we had to swap roles. My heart started thudding. All

155

the wheelbarrows had to be pushers. All the pushers had to be wheelbarrows. I was more like an armoured truck than a wheelbarrow. I was much much much too heavy for Jenny to lift. She tried valiantly but couldn't haul my legs up.

'Don't, Jenny, you'll hurt yourself,' I said, lying on the ground, scarlet as a lobster because everyone was staring at us and sniggering. 'I'm far too flipping *fat*.'

'No, no, it's because my arms aren't strong enough. I haven't got any muscles,' Jenny insisted kindly.

I had another traumatic moment in English. Mrs Marks said we were going to spend the term reading and writing stories about dilemmas and issues, children going through all sorts of problems.

'What, like kids being bullied, Mrs Marks?' Yvonne asked.

'That's certainly one area for us to explore. So why do you think some children are bullied?'

'Because they're wimps?'

'Because they look weird?'

'Because they're *fat*?'

I felt the whole class looking at me. I stared straight ahead, wanting to die.

'There's a Jenna Williams book all about bullying, Mrs Marks,' Jenny said quickly. '*The Girl Gang*. Please can we all read it? It's got all sorts of dilemmas and issues in it.'

'You girls and your Jenna Williams books,' said Mrs Marks. 'Isn't it time you branched out and read something else? Still, you can choose bullying as your homework topic, Jenny, and write me a book report on *The Girl Gang*.'

'Can I do it too, Mrs Marks?' said Yvonne.

'And Emily?' said Jenny.

I smiled at her gratefully, but I wanted to do my own topic.

'The dilemma of being a girl obsessed by a glove puppet?' said Yvonne.

'Oh, ha ha,' I said.

'So what do you want to do, Em?' Jenny asked.

'Oh, just stuff about dads,' I mumbled. 'Well, what it's like when your dad isn't always there.'

Jenny patted my knee understandingly.

'I bet there's a Jenna Williams story about that,' said Yvonne.

'Yep, *Piggy in the Middle*.'

It was about a girl called Candy whose mum and dad split up and they kept arguing over who was to look after her. Candy had this cute little toy piglet called Turnip that she took everywhere with her.

I'd read it at least five times so I could write a book report straight away. I wrote four whole pages. Then I drew a picture of Candy and her mum and her new family and her dad and his new family. I even did a picture of Turnip in his own little shoebox sty.

'You're a very quick reader, Emily,' said Mrs Marks, when I handed my report in the very next day. 'I tell you what, why don't we find you a few more books about children going through the same situation as Candy in *Piggy in the Middle*.'

She started sorting through the classroom shelf of children's classics, the ones that no one ever looks at, let alone reads.

'No one ever got divorced back in olden times,' I said.

'No, they didn't get divorced, but families still split up, or children lost their fathers in some sad

157

way,' said Mrs Marks. 'Try reading *A Little Princess*, Emily, I think you'll enjoy it. Then there's *Little Women* and *The Railway Children*.'

I brightened a little. 'I've seen the film,' I said. 'I like it a lot. But isn't the book a bit old-fashioned and hard to read?'

'Why not give it a try and find out?' said Mrs Marks.

Yvonne pulled a horrified face when she saw I'd been given three classics to read. 'You do your homework quicker than anyone and yet you get *punished* for it?' she said. 'You poor thing, Em!'

Even Jenny looked appalled. But I found I got sucked straight into the story of *The Railway Children*. After a page or two it was just as easy to read as Jenna Williams and I didn't mind a bit that it was old-fashioned. It was a bit weird knowing that Bobbie was fourteen and yet she didn't wear make-up or high heels, she dressed just like a little girl. She didn't *act* like one. Bobbie and Phyllis and Peter were allowed to wander all over the countryside by themselves and their mother didn't worry one bit.

The bits about their father interested me the most. I thought the children were a bit slow to catch on when it was obvious he'd been taken away to prison. I wondered how I'd feel if Dad was in prison. At least I'd be able to visit him once a month, and I'd be able to send him letters and phone him.

It was so awful not knowing where he was. I looked at a map of Britain in an atlas at school. Scotland didn't look very big on the page. I hoped you might be able to search all over in a week or so, but when I asked Mrs Marks she said it was hundreds of miles wide and long. Dad could be up Edinburgh Castle or wandering down Sauchiehall Street or crossing the Tay Road Bridge; he could be sailing across a loch or climbing a mountain or paddling in the sea or patting a Highland cow or playing the bagpipes or wearing a kilt . . .

The sisters in *Little Women* didn't know where their father was either. He was away for most of the book, fighting in a war. I couldn't ever imagine our dad fighting. He was a total pacifist and believed all wars were wicked. Meg, Jo, Beth and Amy were very proud of their dad though, and knitted him socks—just like me knitting Dad his stripy scarf! I wondered if he was still wearing it. Probably not, as it was getting too hot. I hoped he wouldn't just throw it away. If he'd stuffed it in a drawer somewhere, did he take it out sometimes and hold it to his cheek and think of me? Did he ever think about Vita, his little princess? Did he ever wonder how Maxie was managing without him?

The March sisters' dad came back home after he was wounded in battle. If our dad got ill, would he come back to us? I couldn't imagine Sarah doing any nursing.

There was a lot about illness in *Little Women*. I liked the chapter where Beth nearly died. I read it over and over again. If Vita became dangerously ill I'd nurse her devotedly and spoon-feed her and comb her hair and wipe her fevered brow with a cold flannel and tell her endless Dancer stories.

Then I read *A Little Princess*. That was the best book of all, though it was so so sad. I loved the beginning when Sara's father bought her trunkfuls of beautiful clothes—silks and furs as if she really

159

was a little princess. Then Sara's china doll—
Emily!—got kitted out with little cut-down versions
of each outfit. I hated it when he left Sara at the
girls' school and she missed him so much, but the
worst bit of all was when she found out he'd died.

I could bear it if I got so poor I had to work as a
servant or live in an attic like poor Sara, but I
simply couldn't stand it if Dad ever died.

I so identified with Sara that I wore one of
Mum's old black T-shirts and her black skirt (I had
to use a safety pin to do the waistband up—it's
terrible when you're much fatter than your own
mother). I trudged about in my last year's winter
boots, holding my head high, pretending to be a
princess even though I looked like a ragamuffin. I
wore Dancer on my hand, pretending she was a
very big pet rat.

'For pity's sake, what do you look like, Em?' said
Gran.

I gave her a silent look of contempt. This was
the way Sara dealt with Miss Minchin and it always
unsettled her. It *infuriated* Gran.

'Don't you look down your nose at me, Emily!
Take those awful black clothes off. And get rid of
that wretched reindeer! You're too old to go round
clutching a silly soft toy all the time.'

'Dancer isn't a toy, she's a puppet,' I said.

'It isn't even *your* puppet, miss.'

'Vita doesn't mind me borrowing her. She *likes* it
when I make her talk to us.'

'I haven't seen you letting Vita borrow *your*
Christmas present,' said Gran.

'She'd only lose it,' said Mum. 'She's not careful
like Em. Quit nagging at her.' Mum put her arm
round me and whispered 'Take no notice' in

my ear.

I waited until night-time and then when Mum came to tuck me up I hung onto her, pulling her down on the bed beside me.

'Hey, hey, careful, chickie!' said Mum.

'Mum, why does Gran always get at me?'

'She gets at all of us, Em. I told you, she's tired, and she's at a funny age. Try not to let it bother you. I switch off when she's having a go at me and sing a song in my head. You try it some time.'

'I know Gran gets grumpy with all of us . . . but she's meaner to me than Vita or Maxie. I just get on her nerves all the time. She acts like she can't stand me.'

'Oh, darling, don't be silly. Gran loves you, she loves all of us.'

'She doesn't love me like she loves Vita and Maxie,' I said. I pulled Mum's head close beside me on the pillow. 'Is it because I'm fat?' I whispered.

'Oh, Em!' Mum's voice cracked as if she was going to start crying. 'You're not *fat*, sweetheart. You're just going through a little podgy stage.'

'Like I've been in a podgy stage all my *life*. Look at those baby photos of me. I look like a sumo wrestler!'

'Rubbish!'

'I still look like a sumo wrestler now. It's so unfair, when you're all so weeny. Especially you, Mum.' I seized hold of her bony little wrist with my big pink sausage fingers. It felt like it could snap as easily as a wishbone.

'You're so skinny now, Mum. You're not ill, are you?'

'No, of course not.'

161

'Are you sure? Oh, Mum, I do worry about you.'

'You're just my sweet little worrypot. You mustn't worry so, Em. You're just a little girl. I'm the mum. It's my job to worry, not yours. Here, where's Dancer?' Mum put Dancer on and made her tickle my neck with her antlers.

'Cheer up, Em! How about a smile, eh? You need a bit of *fun* in your life.'

*   *   *

It was May Day Monday the next week. Vita, Maxie and I were off school. Mum and Gran had a holiday from work.

'There's a Green Fair in Kingtown,' said Mum. 'Shall we go and see what it's like?'

'A *Green* Fair?' I said. I imagined emerald roundabouts and jade giant wheels and olive dodgems, peppermint candyfloss and sage chips and apple ice cream. 'Like everything's green? Wow!'

'Will you talk *English*, Em?' said Gran. 'Don't be so soft, of course it's not coloured green. More mud-brown, if you ask me.'

'It's green because it's an environmentally friendly fair,' said Mum.

'Full of hippies and gypsies and druggies and drunks,' Gran sniffed. 'You're off your head wanting to take the kids. I don't know what's the matter with you. I did my level best to bring you up decently and yet you run off with the first weirdo who comes along—'

'Mum!'

'And look where that got you—not even able to go to college, and lumbered with a baby, and *then*

162

you fall for Frankie Fly-by-Night and land yourself with more kids, and you won't even work in a decent hairdressing salon, you end up in a crumbling dump like the Pink Palace.'

'The Palace isn't a dump, it's lovely,' I said.

'Can we dress up as hippies and gypsies?' said Vita. 'Can I wear lots of jewellery, my bead necklace and my bunny brooch and my sparkly tiara and my Indian bangles? You can wear Dancer, Em, if you let me wear your emerald ring.'

'Some nasty druggie thief will have that ring off your finger in five seconds,' said Gran.

Maxie was trying to juggle his teddy bears. He couldn't catch even one teddy but he kept throwing them in the air enthusiastically.

'I'm going on the helter-skelter,' he said, out of the blue.

'I'm not sure there'll be a helter-skelter, darling,' said Mum. 'But there'll be lots of other lovely things, food stalls and face painting and lots of music. There might even be juggling. How would you like to try a special juggling workshop?'

'I can juggle already,' said Maxie. 'I want to go on a *helter-skelter*!'

'I want this, I want that! Whatever happened to *Please may I*?' said Gran. 'It's madness taking the children to this godforsaken fair, especially with Maxie in one of his moods. We need to go shopping. All three kids could do with new shoes, though I suppose I'm the one who's got to fork out for them.'

'It's very kind of you, Mum, but I think the children can wait for their shoes,' said Mum, trying to keep her voice steady. 'You go shopping by all means, but *we're* going to the Green Fair.'

163

I wondered if Mum would back down at the last minute, but she organized us into getting ready, leaving the emerald ring hidden at home but letting Dancer come with us.

'She has to. She's part of the family,' said Mum. 'Say goodbye to your gran, everyone.'

We said goodbye. Gran sniffed at us. She waited until Mum was opening the front door.

'I know why you're going to this wretched fair,' she called. 'You're such a *fool*, Julie.'

Mum slammed the door behind us with a big bang.

'Interfering old biddy! Why does she have to keep bossing us about all the time?' Dancer said.

Vita and Maxie laughed. Mum tutted at me, but she couldn't help laughing too.

I worked out what Gran meant when we got to the Green Fair. It was heaving with colourful people in rainbow-coloured clothes. A lot of the guys had long hair. Some had dreadlocks, some had ponytails—and several had plaits.

Vita and Maxie clamoured to have their faces painted. Vita chose to be a lilac fairy with flowers on her cheeks. Maxie was an orange stripy tiger.

'What about you, Em?' said Mum.

'No thanks, it's just for little kids,' I said.

'You *are* my little kid,' said Mum.

'And you're my little mum,' I said, putting my arm round her tiny waist. I kept holding her. 'Mum, Dad's in Scotland now.'

'Yes. He is. Well, as far as we know,' said Mum.

'Are you hoping he might be here, even so?'

'Of course not,' said Mum, but she went pink in the face. 'For goodness' sake don't say anything to Vita or Maxie! No, Dad won't be here, that's a mad

164

idea. Though he did always come to the Green Fair when it was on, and he even talked about trying a Fairyland stall here. You know how he loves this sort of thing.'

I tried to love the Green Fair too, but it didn't have the right sort of fair food. It was all tofu and couscous and grated carrot with weird watery coconut milk to drink.

It didn't have the right sort of fair rides either. There was no helter-skelter. There were no dodgems or big wheels or roundabouts. There were tyres on ropes hanging from trees instead of swings, but they weren't much use to us. Vita and Maxie were so little and skinny they'd have fallen straight through the hole, and I was so big and fat I worried I'd poke my head and shoulders through and then get stuck for ever.

I liked a stall of semi-precious stones. I stayed there for ages, fingering the smooth agate and amethyst and crystal pebbles while the stallholder told me they'd bring me love and luck and happiness. I wanted them all.

'You don't need *semi*-precious stones, Em,' said Mum. 'You've got your very own emerald safe at home.'

I squeezed Mum's hand. I thought hard about my emerald. My head filled with its intense green light. 'Please please please grant me love and luck and happiness,' I wished inside my head.

I opened my eyes, almost believing I'd find Dad there in front of me. I turned my head from side to side, my eyes swivelling over the crowds, searching for him.

Mum was looking round too. Then she stood still, her eyes wide, her mouth parting.

'Mum? Mum, what is it? Have you seen Dad?' I asked, shaking her arm.

I couldn't see any sign of him. Mum seemed to be staring at a family by the children's tent. There was a massive guy in a black vest, his big jeans buckled under his beer belly. He had long coarse yellow hair past his shoulders and a face the colour of tinned ham. He was helping his tubby little toddler son to ride a trike, bent over so that you could see too much of his horrible wobbly bottom. His skinny dark wife had a fat baby riding on her hip, guzzling juice from a bottle.

The big fat guy was staring back at Mum. Then he waved his big beefy arm and started striding across the grass towards us.

'Who's this man, Mum? Do you know him?' I asked.

Mum swallowed. 'Oh, Em. It's your dad.'

I looked at Mum like she'd gone crazy. How could Mum think this massive meaty man could possibly be Dad?

Then I realized. He was my *real* dad.

'Let's run, Mum, quick,' I said.

I'd been too little when we did a runner to remember what he looked like. Mum had long since torn up all the photos. But I couldn't forget the threat of his voice, the thump of his blows, the sound of Mum screaming.

I grabbed Mum's arm and pulled. She was standing as if her silver sandals had grown roots and she was planted for ever in the muddy turf.

'It's Julie! By God, it really is!' he shouted, marching over to us.

'Who's that man?' Maxie asked, biting his bottom lip.

'How does he know you, Mum?' Vita asked.

'Quick, we're all going to run for it,' I said, but it was too late.

He was standing so close we could smell him. He was grinning, hands on his hips, shaking his head so that his hair rasped on his shoulders.

'I can't believe it! Well, Julie, long time no see.' But he wasn't looking at her, he was looking at Vita, with her painted flower face and her fluffy hair and her pink and lilac little-girly clothes.

'Is this little fairy my Emily?' he said.

'I'm not Em!' Vita said indignantly. *'That's* Em.' She pointed at me.

My dad took a proper look at me and then burst out laughing. 'Of course you're Emily!' he said. 'How could I have mixed you up? Talk about a chip off the old block!'

I was appalled. I didn't really look like this big fat ugly dad, did I? Oh God, I did, I did. I shrank as his big blubbery hand reached out and squeezed my shoulder.

'My, you've grown up, kiddo. I can't believe it! So who's the fairy and the little gnome, Julie?'

'They're my other kids, Barry,' Mum said shakily.

'I'm not a gnome, I'm a tiger. I'll bite you if you don't watch out,' Maxie threatened.

I grabbed hold of him but the big guy was just laughing.

'Help! Help! Don't eat me, big tiger,' he said, in a silly squeaky voice. Then he looked at Vita. 'What are you going to do, Magic Fairy? Are you going to wave your wand and grant me a magic wish?'

'No way,' said Vita, folding her arms. 'I'm

keeping all my wishes for me.'

My dad laughed again and looked at Mum. 'Well, your kids do you proud, Julie, all three of them.'

He played silly tricks with Maxie and Vita, pretending he was twisting their noses off, sticking his thumb through his fingers to make them think he'd really done it. They laughed at him scornfully, not the slightest bit frightened. Then he tried it with me, but I dodged out of his way.

'Sorry, sorry!' he said, holding his hands up. 'You're too old for larking about, I know. How did you get to be so grown up, Emily? Dear oh dear, you and me have missed out on a lot. Perhaps we could spend some time together so you can get to know your old dad?'

'I've already got a dad,' I said.

Mum tensed.

'Oh well, I'm glad to hear it,' said my dad, nicely enough. 'So things have worked out for you, Julie?'

Mum nodded, holding my hand tight.

'That's good. I know you and me—well, it didn't work, did it? Maybe I gave you a bit of a rough time.'

'Maybe,' said Mum.

'Still, I'm off the drink now. Regular family man. That's my new lady over there, and my boys, bless the little bruisers. Want to come and meet them?'

'Maybe not,' said Mum.

'Yeah, it's all a bit awkward. Oh well. It was nice seeing you. And I'd like to keep in touch, hear about my Emily. Where are you living now?'

Mum hesitated.

'At Gran's,' Maxie blurted out.

My dad pulled a silly face. 'Oh dear! Perhaps I'd

better keep my distance. We were never the best of friends!'

He waved his fat fingers at us and then ambled back to his new family.

'Thank God he's gone!' Mum whispered.

'Is that man really Em's dad? I thought Em's dad was a really scary man?' said Vita.

'He is,' said Mum. 'Well, he was. I don't know. Maybe he's changed.'

'I don't like him,' said Maxie. 'He took my nose.'

'I don't like him either,' I said. 'Come on, let's all walk the other way, quick.'

'Our dad's much nicer than Em's dad,' said Vita.

'That's enough, Vita,' said Mum sharply. She put her arm round me. 'Don't worry, sweetheart,' she said. 'He's gone now. We'll never see him again. Come on, there's an ice-cream van over there. Proper Whippy ice cream. I'll treat us all to a ninety-nine.'

I had a large cone with strawberry sauce and rainbow sprinkles and two chocolate flakes. I caught sight of myself reflected in the van window as I had my first long lick. I saw my big pink face, my fat sausage fingers. I stopped licking. I let the ice cream melt until it dripped up my arm. Then I threw it down and trod it into the mud.

Ten

'You didn't see him, did you?' Gran said, when we got home.

'We didn't see *my* dad, but we saw Em's!' said Vita.

Gran thought she was making it up at first. Then she got furious with Mum.

'You mean you didn't pin him down about making maintenance payments for Em? For pity's sake, Julie, what are you like? There was a golden opportunity. Why do you let all these awful guys in your life walk all over you? Why won't you try to screw them for everything you can get? I know that pig doesn't give a damn about his own daughter, but he's her father and he should pay for her.'

'Stop getting at Mum, Gran,' I said. 'My dad *does* give a damn, he wanted to take me out, so there! But I don't want to so I don't have to, do I, Mum?'

'That's right, darling,' said Mum.

'Oh yes, that's right, you all do what you want. What about me? When can I do what *I* want?' said Gran. 'I've worked hard all my life. I've managed on my own. I've brought you up single-handed, Julie. Just when I've got to the time of life when I thought I could ease off, have a bit of fun, take a holiday like anyone else, I'm landed with you and your three kids and I'm the muggins paying all the bills.'

'I'm trying to pay my way, Mum, you know I am. Once I get the credit cards paid off I'll be able to pay a lot more,' my mum said, her face crumpling.

'Look what you've done, Gran, you've made her cry,' I said furiously.

'Oh, it's easy to give up and burst into tears. Did you see *me* crying when that con-man Frankie stole my savings?'

'He didn't steal them, Mum, he just borrowed them,' Mum sobbed.

'Oh yes, and he'll pay it back? And pay off all your debts too?' Gran glared at Vita and Maxie and me. 'You kids think your dad's such a lovely guy for giving you all these ridiculous treats and presents—and flipping emerald rings! He didn't pay a penny for them. Your mum and I are the poor fools who've ended up forking out for the lot.'

'Shut up, Gran! My dad *is* lovely,' Vita yelled. 'I looked and looked and looked for him at the Green Fair and it's so mean, because Em got to see her dad and I want *mine*.' She started shouting it over and over again, almost having a Maxie-type tantrum. He was crying too, just so he wouldn't be overlooked.

'There! I told you going to the stupid Green Fair was a silly idea. The kids have got all worked up and over-excited,' said Gran.

I wondered if she knew how much she twisted things round. Did she really think she was right all

174

the time? Did she like making us all feel bad?

I could hear Gran and Mum carrying on rowing all the time I was upstairs with Vita and Maxie. I put Dancer on my hand and told them a long story about the special Snowy White Fairs they have in Lapland. When I came downstairs at last I found Mum and Gran sitting on the sofa together. Mum was still crying but Gran had her arm round her.

'Come here, Em,' said Gran, holding out her other arm. 'Come and have a cuddle.'

'No thanks,' I said, sitting on the spare chair instead. I flipped through Gran's *Hello!* magazine as if I couldn't care less.

'Ooh, look at Little Miss Sulky,' said Gran.

I did my best to ignore her. I stared hard at *Hello!*, imagining living in a huge house with white sofas and gold chandeliers and televisions hanging on the walls like a painting. I pretended Dad was a truly famous movie star and Mum had her own chic chain of hairdressing salons and I was their thin-as-a-pin daughter, sitting at their feet and smiling sweetly at the camera.

'What are you smirking at, Em?' said Gran.

My smile soured to a scowl. I still didn't say a single word. I didn't even say goodnight when I went up to bed.

Mum waited until Vita and Maxie were asleep and then she crept in to see me. She eased Vita over to the other side of the bed and slipped under the covers with me.

'Gran's sorry, Em.'

'She didn't say so.'

'No, well, she doesn't ever *say* sorry, you know that. But she knows she went too far.'

'I hate her,' I said.

'No you don't.'

'She hates me!'

'Of course she doesn't. She loves you. She loves all of us. That's why she gets so worked up. She's not really cross with us, she's cross with your dad. *Both* your dads!' Mum gave a little sniff. 'It was so weird seeing your real dad again, Em. He seems so different now. Maybe he was just horrible with us. He looked like he was happy with that other woman and the little boys. I'm sure he doesn't batter them.'

Mum sniffed again. I felt her cheeks in the dark to see if she was crying.

'Don't be scared, Mum. If he comes round to batter us we'll call the police, quick.'

'I'm not worried about that, love. No, I'm just thinking, maybe there's something about me that makes men go funny. Maybe I'm just a useless partner.'

'You're a brilliant partner, Mum. You didn't make him horrid to us. He was just mean and he wanted to shout and scare us. He *hit* us,' I said. 'Mum, I *wish* he wasn't my real dad.'

'He wasn't all bad, pet. Maybe you'd like him if you got to know him now.'

I wanted to think he was totally bad. I didn't want to like him. I loved my *new* dad—even though he'd gone off and left us.

'I'm never ever living with any man,' I said.

'That's silly, pet. You can't say that just because things haven't worked out for me.'

'No one would have me anyway!'

'Of course they would! You're a lovely lovely girl.'

'All the boys at school think I'm rubbish. They

call me Fatso and The Blob and they all puff out their cheeks, imitating me.'

'Oh darling, that's horrible.'

'It's OK. I call them names back. But I am a Fatso Blob. I take after my real dad, don't I?'

'You're not a bit like your dad. You're a sweet kind gentle caring girl.'

'I *look* like him. If I wore a black vest and jeans I'd be just like a little replica.'

'You're *nothing* like him,' Mum lied. 'You're not like him, you're not like me. You're *you*, my lovely Em. I think it's rot we're all supposed to take after our parents. I certainly don't want to be like Gran!' Mum paused. 'For pity's sake, Julie,' she said, in Gran's thin whiny voice.

We both burst out laughing. Vita woke up and sleepily complained that we were shaking the bed and would we please stop now, immediately.

'I think *Vita* takes after Gran,' I whispered to Mum. 'She's bossier than her already.'

*   *   *

Gran nagged just as much the next morning, when we were all rushing off to school and work, but that evening she made us spaghetti bolognese, with strawberries and ice cream for pudding. She gave me an extra scoop of ice cream *and* let me scrape round the empty carton afterwards.

'But it's back on that diet tomorrow, Em, OK?' Gran said.

I did wonder about trying harder. I still mostly chose chips instead of salad at school dinners but I didn't buy secret supplies of Kit-Kat and Mars bars and Smarties with my pocket money now. I still wanted them desperately but I wanted to save all my treat money. I wanted to save up so I could pay Gran some of the money we owed. Then she'd maybe stop moaning.

Mum was trying hard too, taking on as much extra work as she could. The Pink Palace didn't open till midday now because they got so few morning customers. Mum made herself some 'Good Fairy' cards using stationery from leftover Fairyland stock, saying she was willing to fly round to clients' houses and cut and blow-dry their hair between nine and twelve. She started to get booked up most mornings, and she had a special regular job on Wednesdays at an old people's day centre, snipping her way through silvery locks, one old lady after another at a special £5 rate.

'I have to cram as many in as possible, doing them for that rate,' said Mum. 'It's a bit like sheep-shearing. I'll be taking hold of them by their Scholl sandals, throwing them over my shoulder and clipping their perms into crewcuts soon.'

Mum got up even earlier on Saturday mornings, doing special wedding hairdos, often fitting in the bride, chief bridesmaid and the bride's mother before rushing to start her stint at the Palace.

'Imagine if I got mixed up, and dyed all the wedding clients purple and magenta and gave twee mother-of-the-bride shampoo and sets to all the goths at the Palace,' said Mum.

She tried to make a joke of it, but she was so tired now that she fell asleep as soon as she sat down on the sofa when she got home.

'Mum's no fun now,' said Vita. 'She won't make me up like a grown-up lady or play Fairy Queens or do *anything* now, she just falls asleep.'

'Yes, I was telling her about this bad boy who pushed me and she didn't *listen*, her eyes kept closing,' Maxie said indignantly.

'Mum's tired out,' I said. 'Leave her alone. *I'll* make you up and play Fairy Queens with you, Vita. Just let me give Maxie a cuddle first and find out all about this bad boy.'

I knew I had to be very grown up and understanding but *I* wished Mum wasn't so worn out. She was skinnier than ever, with dark circles under her eyes.

Gran was worried about her too.

'You're exhausting yourself, Julie. You don't have to take on quite so many clients. Never mind the blooming money. I wanted your deadbeat missing bloke to pay his debts. I didn't mean *you* should work yourself to death on his behalf.'

'I'm fine, Mum,' Mum murmured, rubbing her forehead and yawning.

'You need a holiday. We all do,' said Gran.

'Yes, well, holidays cost money,' said Mum. 'We'll have to make do this year. Maybe I'll be able to take the kids on a day out here and there.'

I started to think and think and think about a summer holiday. Jenny was going to the seaside in France, ending up with a day in EuroDisney. Yvonne was going to Spain for a week with her mum, and CenterParcs for three days with her dad.

I couldn't help daydreaming for days about Dad inviting us on holiday with him. We didn't have to go *away* anywhere. We'd have been happy to stay in one room with him (just so long as Sarah wasn't there too).

I kept thinking of that evening at the seaside. It sparkled in my mind like the fairy lights on the end of the pier. I wondered what would have happened if we'd stayed the night like Dad suggested. Would he have kept us? Sometimes, when Mum was tired and Gran was snappy, I'd wish and wish we could live with Dad instead.

Then I'd feel desperately guilty and try harder than ever to be good to Mum. I didn't always try to be good to *Gran*.

'I *wish* I could take Mum on holiday,' I whispered to Dancer.

'Lapland's pretty in the summer,' she said.

'I'd like to take Mum somewhere really warm and sunny so she'd lie and sunbathe and get brown and look happy again,' I said.

'You could try wishing,' said Dancer.

I took my hand out of her head and looked at my beautiful emerald ring. I held it up so that it caught the light and wished as hard as I could.

Then I looked at the ring again.

I kept on looking at it.

I wondered how much emerald rings cost. Dad said he'd bought it second hand, but Mum and Gran said they thought it was still worth hundreds of pounds.

If I had hundreds of pounds we could all go on holiday.

I thought about it day after day. I loved my emerald ring so much. It was the best present in the whole world. I wasn't allowed to wear it very often. Obviously I couldn't wear it to school, and Mum didn't like me wearing it outside just in case I lost it. I wore it at home whenever I could, but mostly it was kept in its little box, hidden in my knicker drawer in case of burglars.

I couldn't bear the thought of selling it so that

I'd lost it for ever. But maybe, just maybe, I could *pawn* it?

I'd read about pawn shops in one of my favourite Jenna Williams books, *The Victorian Project*. I knew loads and loads of poor people pawned their rings and their watches and even their best Sunday suits back in olden times. I wasn't sure you could still pawn things nowadays.

There was an old jewellery shop in an alley by the market place. It had three golden balls hanging above its doorway. It *used* to be a pawn shop. Maybe it still was one. And *maybe* it might be interested in my beautiful emerald ring.

I didn't know how I would ever raise the money to get it back again, but at least it wouldn't be selling it for ever. Maybe they'd display it in the window so I could go and look at it.

I got my chance the very next Saturday, when Mum was doing a wedding and then going on to the Palace. Gran had to take Vita, Maxie and me into town to buy new sandals. We all needed them badly. I was still stomping around in my big lace-up winter shoes. They were so small for me I felt like I was lacing my toes into corsets every time I tied them up. Vita was wearing her winter buckle shoes too. My last year's sandals were still way too big for her, and she insisted she'd sooner go barefoot than wear my horrible scuffed cast-offs anyway. Maxie had Vita's old sandals and he didn't mind wearing them one bit, but they were pink jelly plastic. Maxie adored them but when he wore them to school everyone said they were girls' shoes and sniggered at him.

It was a very long and fraught morning. Gran lost her temper, Maxie howled, Vita sobbed and I

181

despaired, because my new flat black sandals were so big they looked like flippers.

'For pity's sake, what a fuss!' said Gran. 'Let's go up to the food court and have a cup of tea. I'll treat all three of you to a cake if you'll only shut up, the lot of you.'

'Um, Gran, you said shut up!' said Maxie.

'Can't we go down to McDonald's instead? I want a McFlurry ice cream,' said Vita.

My mouth was watering at the thought of cake *or* ice cream, but this was my big chance.

'I'm not going to have anything. I want to stick to my diet,' I said.

'That's the ticket, Em,' said Gran, looking surprised.

'But it's torture watching everyone else eat, so please may I go and look at the bears being made in the Bear Factory while you're in the food court?'

Gran hesitated. 'Well, if you promise you'll go straight there and not talk to any strangers and then come right back here in fifteen minutes . . . then OK,' said Gran. 'Only take that blooming glove puppet off your hand—you look gormless, a great big girl like you.'

'No, Dancer wants to see the bears too,' I said. 'Don't you, Dancer? You want to see the special bear ballet dancers with their pink satin shoes, isn't that right?'

I made Dancer nod emphatically, her antlers waving in the air.

'It's not fair, she's *my* puppet,' said Vita.

'Yes, give her back to Vita,' said Gran, but she was distracted by Maxie screaming at the escalators.

I dashed off before she could stop me. If I took

Dancer off she'd see I was wearing the emerald ring on my finger. I wanted Dancer's company anyway. It felt a bit weird and scary going right out of the Flowerfields shopping centre and over to the market place. I knew Gran would kill me if she ever found out.

I ran all the way to the jewellery shop, my heart thumping. I checked on the one, two, three golden balls dangling above the door. I wasted two of my precious minutes pretending to look at the window display, too scared to step inside.

'Go *on*,' said Dancer, and she put her front hooves on the handle and pulled the door open.

I stood in the middle of the shop while fifty clocks ticked and tocked at me all around the room. An old man and a young man stood at either side, behind counters. The young man sighed at the sight of me, but the old man cocked his head on one side and looked obliging.

'Can I help you, young lady?' he said.

'I hope so.' I moved towards him, trying to tug Dancer off. My hand was so hot and sticky it was a struggle. 'Is this a pawn shop?'

'Well, we do offer a loan service. But not to children, I'm afraid,' said the old man.

I thought quickly. 'Oh, this isn't for me. This is for my mum. She's too embarrassed to come herself. She wants to know how much she'd get if she pawned this emerald ring.' I peeled the last piece of Dancer off and flapped my hot hand in the air, flourishing my beautiful emerald. Its green glow sparkled all around the room.

The young man clucked his teeth. 'Does your mum know you've got her ring?' he said.

'Of course she does, I *said*. Do you think I'm a

liar?' I said, getting hotter and hotter.

'May I see the ring?' said the old man, still courteous.

I had to lick my finger until it was slippery enough to ease the ring off. The old man took hold of it gingerly. He held it to the light. Then he shook his head at me.

'Why don't you go home and stop wasting our time,' he said.

'What do you mean? Won't you take my emerald—*Mum's* emerald?'

'It isn't an emerald. It's green glass in a gilt setting. You used to be able to buy them in Woolworths for a shilling. It's not worth much more now.'

'Funny joke, dear,' said the young man, poker-faced.

'It's not a joke. It *is* an emerald, I know it is. My dad got it from an antique fair. I know he paid heaps of money for it,' I gabbled.

'Then he was conned, dear,' said the old man, handing me my emerald back. My fingers closed over it protectively.

I ran out of the shop. I heard them laughing behind me.

I poked my finger into my poor ring, clutched Dancer and ran. Tears pricked my eyes. When I got to the Flowerfields shopping centre I took deep breaths, trying to stop snivelling.

'There there, sweetheart,' said Dancer, wiping my eyes tenderly. 'Take no notice of those idiots. *They're* the con men. They were probably just trying to trick you out of your emerald. Of *course* it's real.'

I looked at it on my finger. Just for a moment its

green glow dulled. I saw a chip of coloured glass stuck in cheap gilt, a Christmas cracker ring.

Dancer changed her tactics. 'It's the same ring Dad gave you, so it's the most special ring in the world whether it's a real emerald or not. And I say it *is* real. As real as you and me.'

I hugged her and looked at the ring again. Its glow was back, glittering green.

I got back to Gran and Vita and Maxie just as Gran was looking at her watch and frowning.

'You're two minutes late,' she said. 'Come on, now, Maxie's desperate for a wee and we'll have to take him to the ladies with us.'

'You ran off with *my* Dancer,' said Vita, frowning. 'But I still saved you half my cake.'

She'd licked all the icing off, but it was still sweet of her.

'Did you *really* go to the Bear Factory?' said Vita, while Gran was mopping up Maxie and his damp dungarees. 'I peered over the balcony railings and I thought I saw you on the escalator.'

'It must have been somebody else,' I said—like there were *lots* of big fat girls in too-tight jeans and a fairy T-shirt with a reindeer glove puppet on their right hand.

I didn't want to tell Vita about the jewellery shop. It was too awful and embarrassing. There was no point anyway. I couldn't take us on holiday after all.

*   *   *

But Gran could. The day we all broke up from school Gran made us wait for tea till Mum came home. Then she sent out for a giant pizza, opened

185

a bottle of wine for her and Mum, with Coke for us kids.

'What are we celebrating?' said Mum.

'The start of the summer holidays,' I said.

'I wish we were *going* on holiday,' said Vita.

'Let's go to the seaside. The seaside with the helter-skelter,' said Maxie.

'Ssh, Maxie, Vita. We can't go away on holiday, you know we can't,' I said.

'Yes we can!' said Gran. She opened up her handbag and produced a little folder of tickets. 'It's all booked up. We're going to Spain for a week, all five of us, staying in a great big hotel by the sea.'

'With a helter-skelter?' Maxie persisted.

Vita whooped with excitement. I whooped too, but I felt wrong-footed.

'But Mum, how on earth have you managed it?' said our mum, looking dazed.

'Never you mind. I just felt we all badly needed a holiday,' said Gran. 'Now simmer down, kids.'

We couldn't simmer. We were boiling over with excitement. Vita started dancing round the room, showing us her version of Spanish dancing. Dancer demonstrated too, doing a mid-air flamenco. I stamped my foot in time. Maxie gave up on the helter-skelter and jumped wildly up and down.

'For pity's sake, mind my—' said Gran. Then she stopped in mid sentence.

I looked over at the china cabinet. There was something the matter. The little pink crinoline lady was spreading her skirt in solitary splendour on the top shelf. Where was the balloon seller and the little mermaid and the children in their white china nightgowns?

'Gran, your china!' I gasped.

186

'Has someone stolen it?' said Vita.

'Stolen!' said Maxie fearfully.

'Don't be so silly,' Gran snapped. 'I decided to weed out a few pieces. They were just gathering dust, no use to anyone.'

'Oh, Mum, you loved your china collection!' said our mum. 'You sold it to pay for our holiday. It's so sweet of you.'

Mum gave Gran a big hug. I couldn't help feeling jealous. *I'd* so wanted to take everyone on holiday by pawning my emerald ring.

'Did you pawn your china, Gran?' I asked.

'Did I *what*?' said Gran. 'No, of course not, I sold it in the antique centre. Honestly, Em, where do you get all these silly ideas from?'

'They're not silly! If you pawn things you can get them back again when you've got enough money,' I said. 'Why do you *always* have to say I'm silly?'

'Hey, hey, that's enough, Em. Don't cheek your gran, especially when she's done such a lovely thing for us,' said Mum sharply.

I started to get seriously fed up with this holiday as the weeks went by. I had to act eternally grateful to Gran. She traded on it too. Every time I moaned when she told me to wash up or I argued over what I wanted to watch on the television or I locked myself into the bathroom to write my Dancer story, Gran would threaten me.

'You'll do those dishes because I say so. Vita's too young, she'd only break them. Now make yourself useful or you won't go on holiday!'

'We're not watching *The Bill*, it's not suitable. Just because your dad was in it once doesn't make it compulsory viewing for the rest of us. Now take that sulky look off your face or you won't go on holiday.'

'What on earth are you up to in there, Emily? For pity's sake, come out of the bathroom at once! You watch it, young lady, or you won't go on holiday.'

I decided I didn't *want* to go on holiday. I'd stay at home by myself and eat chocolate bars all day long and watch whatever I wanted on the telly and read all my Jenna Williams books and write my Dancer story in perfect peace.

Eleven

I didn't stay at home. I went on holiday with Mum and Gran and Vita and Maxie. I actually had a fabulous time! The hotel was a big white tower overlooking the sea. Our two rooms were right at the very top, which was a bit of a problem. Maxie kicked and screamed at the very idea of going in the glass lift.

Gran got cross and tried giving him a good talking to. Maxie got crosser still and screamed back. Mum tried bribing him with sweets. Maxie swallowed them quickly but still refused to step into the lift.

'So what are we going to do? March up twelve flipping flights of stairs?' Gran said.

'I'll walk up the stairs with him,' I said.

'Don't be so silly, Em. You couldn't get up *one* flight without huffing and puffing,' said Gran.

'I'm not being silly,' I said, through gritted teeth. 'Come on, Maxie, I'll take you. We'll race up those stairs, won't we?'

We raced up the first flight of stairs. Then we slowed down a little. My heart was thumping a bit

191

but I *wasn't* huffing and puffing. We went up the second flight and the third. Maxie hung on my hand, dragging his feet.

'Come on, Maxie, keep going,' I said.

'Don't want to. I'm tired,' Maxie said, flopping down on the stairs.

'Do you want to try the lift again?'

'No!'

'Then it's stairs or nothing.' I bent over him, feeling the sharp little bones sticking out at the back of his T-shirt. 'Are these wings? Yes, they are! They'll help you fly up. Come on, Maxie, we'll fly like Peter Pan. Wheeee! Wheeee!'

We 'flew' for another couple of flights. Then we both had to have a little sit down. Maxie put his head on his knees.

'It's too high up,' he moaned.

'Yes, it is, ever so high. Let's pretend it's a mountain and we're climbing way way up to the very top. When we get there we'll plant a flag on the summit and get filmed for television.'

'Like the special videos?' said Maxie.

We had three special videos of Dad. One was his proper speaking part in *The Bill*. The second was an *EastEnders* market crowd scene where Dad gets to smile and wave though he doesn't actually say anything, The third was an advert for a mobile phone. That always made me cry because I kept remembering Dad in the kitchen at Christmas. I still watched it though. When Dad first left at Christmas I watched the videos over and over, every single day. I still watched them at least once a week. So did Mum and Vita. Maxie never *seemed* to be watching, but he was often in the room.

I put my arms round him. 'I was just pretending,

192

Maxie,' I said. 'We're not *really* going to be filmed. Gran's brought her camera though, so we'll have photos of us on holiday. We'll take a photo of you looking all cute in your new shorts and your big boy's baseball cap, yeah?'

'Mmm,' said Maxie, his chin still on his knees.

'Are you thinking about Dad, Maxie?' I whispered.

Maxie shook his head, but I knew he was.

'Dad would give you a ride on his back up the stairs, wouldn't he?' I said. 'But *I* can't, Maxie. I just can't manage to carry you. I want someone to carry *me*! But we're going to get up these stupid stairs just to show Gran, right?'

'Right,' said Maxie.

He stood up, flexing his little arms. Then he tried to take hold of me.

'What are you doing? Hey, that tickles!'

'I'm trying to carry you,' Maxie said.

'Oh Maxie, you're so sweet! You could never ever ever pick up a big fat lump like me,' I said. 'Come on, we'll hold hands and take turns helping each other, right?'

We climbed on upwards—and met Mum, rushing down to find us, worried we'd collapsed on the way.

Vita had already taken charge of the bedroom, commandeering the entire double bed, and all of the chest of drawers, spreading out her T-shirts and shorts and fairy dress and disco-dancing costume so that each drawer had one garment. She insisted that Dancer wanted the little single bed all to herself too.

There's one advantage of being the big sister—especially when you're a *very* big sister. In two

193

minutes Vita had been thoroughly vanquished and squashed until she begged for mercy, and I had allocated the bedroom more fairly. Vita was left with half the double bed and *one* drawer. Dancer stayed in her single bed because Maxie pulled the mattress off, made a cave and huddled there quite happily with his tattered teddies. (We'd had to bring them with us, in a bulging laundry bag.)

We had our very own en suite bathroom. We tried the shower taps to see if they were working. They were working a little too efficiently. Mum just laughed when she saw us.

'Never mind! Let's go and check out the swimming pool, seeing as you're all soaked anyway.'

The pool was fantastic, a big turquoise rectangle with green deckchairs and sun loungers spread all around, with a little poolside café in case you got peckish. We spent day after day there, Gran and Mum lying on sun loungers and smoothing on suncream and reading their fat paperbacks, and Vita and Maxie and me having six swims a day. Well, Maxie didn't technically swim. He lay on his tummy in the paddling pool and kicked his legs and pretended he was swimming. Vita got brave enough to come in the big pool with me but she insisted on wearing her inflated armbands and a rubber ring, and she screamed if she ever went under. I was the only one who swam properly.

I'd learned to swim at school. It had been total agony having everyone staring at me in my swimming costume and making horrible comments. I was terribly shy of swimming in public in the hotel pool, even though Mum had bought me a new big blue costume and insisted I looked lovely in it.

'Yeah, like a lovely blue whale,' I said, and made mournful whale whistles.

I thought I'd stick out appallingly but there were a couple of other fat kids who were dashing about in teeny weeny costumes, not seeming at all self-conscious. I tried not to care what I looked like either. I shrugged off my big towelling dressing gown and jumped into the pool.

I discovered something extraordinary. I was good at swimming. I'd only swum widths at school. Now I swam lengths. Once I'd relaxed and got used to it I found I could swim and swim and swim up and down the pool, faster than all the other kids, even faster than a lot of grown-ups!

They'd only taught us breaststroke at school. I wished I knew how to do some other strokes. I watched this nice dad showing his little boy how to do freestyle but the kid was nearly as wimpy as Maxie and kept whining that he was getting water up his nose. I couldn't remember if our dad could swim. I wished he was with us to teach me, standing beside me, smooth and tanned with his pigtail sleek down his brown back.

I tried to copy what the dad was saying. He spotted me windmilling my arms and kicking my legs.

'That's it, love! You've got it. You're a great little swimmer. Here, curve your fingers more, like this.'

He ended up teaching me while his little boy Edward played ball with our Maxie. Neither of them could catch but they had a lot of fun running after each ball.

Edward's dad told Mum and Gran that I was a real little water baby and ought to have proper lessons. Mum gave me a hug and said she was proud of me. Gran asked straight out if Edward had a mum. She looked disappointed when she found out she'd just gone on a shopping trip.

'That's such a shame,' said Gran. 'I thought you'd do just fine for my daughter!'

'Mum!' our mum hissed, mortified.

Mum and Gran had a little row about it later when we were all having ice creams.

'Will you please stop trying to pair me up with someone! It's dead embarrassing. I'm not *interested.*'

'It's no use wasting your life hoping Frankie will come back,' said Gran.

'He *will* come back, he *will* come back, he *will* come back,' I mouthed at Vita.

She nodded and mouthed it back to me.

I counted the cherries in my ice-cream sundae. One—he *will* come back. Two—he won't. Three—he *will* come back. Four—he won't. Five—he *WILL*! I crammed all five cherries into my mouth at once and choked, so that Mum had to thump me on the back.

'Stop being such a greedy-guts, Em. And how many calories are in that ice cream? What about your diet?' said Gran.

'Mum, give it a rest! She's on holiday!' said my mum.

'All right, all right, it's just that it would be a shame to give up on it just as she's doing so well.'

'What do you mean, Gran?' I asked.

'You've lost a bit of weight, love,' said Mum.

'*Have* I?' I said.

I peered down at myself. I still looked horribly blue-whaleish. Maybe there was just a *little* bit less of a tummy. Was this just because I'd stopped

196

eating my secret snacks? How could going without one little chocolate bar—or two, or maybe even three—each day make so much difference? I'd carried on saving up all the money. I hadn't been able to take Mum on holiday but I *could* take her out for a special meal.

'I'm going to take us all out for our dinner,' I announced proudly.

'We don't need to go out,' said Gran. 'We're getting dinner at the hotel. It's already paid for.'

'I want to take us *out* for dinner,' I said. 'I want to buy Mum a special meal for a holiday treat. Look, I've got money, heaps of it. I can change it into euros easy-peasy and pay for it myself.'

I delved into my school bag, scrabbled through my cardie and beach towel and flip-flops, my Dancer notebook and my three favourite Jenna Williams books, and right at the bottom found the fat envelope chinking with gold coins. I shook it like a tambourine.

'For pity's sake, Em, have you robbed a slot machine?' said Gran.

'Oh lovie, you've saved all your treat money! *Months* of it!' said Mum, and she gave me a big hug. OK then, my wonderful generous girl, you take us out for a meal tonight.'

We all changed into our best things after a day's sunbathing and swimming. I wore the only dress I like, a deep green silky shirt-dress that hangs loosely. Mum plaited the top of my hair and tied it with a green velvet ribbon. My emerald sparkled on my finger. Vita sparkled all over in her favourite rainbow disco outfit, and Dancer had pink ribbons tied around her antlers. Maxie wore his baseball cap back to front and wouldn't tuck his shirt into

197

his shorts so he looked cool (well, *he* thought so). Mum wore her white frock with a silver chain belt and her special silver sandals.

Gran scoffed at all of us and said she wasn't going to bother changing, but at the last minute she rushed up to her room. She came down wearing a pink lacy top, pink strappy sandals just as high as Mum's, and the black jeans Dad bought for her at Christmas. She hadn't worn them since. We hadn't known she'd even taken them on holiday.

'What are you all staring at?' Gran said grumpily, but she couldn't help smiling a little bit. She had pink lipstick on too.

'You look pretty, Gran!' said Vita.

'You look like a *lady*!' said Maxie.

'Oh, thanks very much, our Maxie. So I normally look like a *man*, do I?' said Gran, pretending to swat him.

'He means you look a total glamour puss,' said Mum. 'Hey, this is *my* night out. What are you doing upstaging me? You don't look like my mum any more. You look like my sister.' Then Mum smiled at me. 'And you look so gorgeous and grown up in your green dress that you look like my sister *too*, Em.'

It was so lovely to see Mum being all happy and bubbly with her white dress showing off her new tan. I felt thrilled to be giving her a real treat.

I did get a bit worried when we walked along the beach road into town and couldn't find a good place to eat. There were lots of burger and chip places with special menus in English but they were all a bit noisy and messy and Gran got sniffy about holidaymakers who didn't have the sense to sample the local cuisine.

When we got near the fish market there were lots more restaurants displaying plates of squid and octopus with wriggly slimy tentacles, and huge weird slabs of fish with scary faces. Gran shut up sharpish, because this food was a bit *too* local for any of us.

We trudged on to the posh end of town and found a proper restaurant, all white linen tablecloths and flowers on the table and waiters in evening clothes.

'This looks a lovely place, Mum!' I said, clutching her arm.

'Hang on a tick. Let's look at the menu,' said Mum.

I peered round a fat man in a blue shirt and squinted at the menu. It was all in Spanish, but I could understand the prices. My heart started thudding. I'd thought I was so rich—but I didn't have enough to pay for *one* meal, let alone five.

'I think it looks a horrible uncomfy snobby sort of place. I'd *hate* to go there,' Mum said quickly.

'Well, where *are* we going to go?' said Gran. She looked at her watch. 'We could rush back to the hotel. We've missed the starters but they'll probably still serve us the main course.'

'I don't mind just having pudding,' said Vita.

'Pudding!' said Maxie. 'I want pudding!' He rubbed his tummy emphatically.

'Ssh, kids, we're all going to have pudding, *and* a main course too—but this is my special night *out*,' said Mum, steering Vita and Maxie out of the fat man's way. He smiled at Vita and rubbed his tummy back at Maxie.

'We've just got to find somewhere nice to eat, that's all,' I said, trying to sound positive.

'Well, we've been looking long enough,' said Gran. She wiggled her foot out of her pink strappy sandal and rubbed a sore toe, wincing. 'It's obvious we're not going to stumble across somewhere cheap but decent by chance. If only we could speak a bit of Spanish, then we could ask someone.'

The fat man turned round to us and pointed at himself enquiringly. Gran was taken by surprise and wobbled on one foot. He caught her quickly by the elbow and steadied her.

'Thank you!' she said. 'Sorry—*gracias, señor.*'

'You're very welcome,' said the fat man, his blue eyes twinkling.

'You speak wonderful English,' said Gran, shoving her sandal back on.

'I should hope so. I *am* English, though I've lived here for several years now. I was eavesdropping shamelessly. I think I know the perfect place for you all to have a lovely relaxed meal. It's a real family restaurant, and they'll make a big fuss of the children. It's only down the next alleyway and round the corner. Shall I show you?'

'How very sweet of you. Yes please!' said Gran.

She started chatting away to him while we trooped along behind. We heard Gran asking if his family all lived in Spain too. She made attentive cooing sounds of sympathy when he said his wife had died a year ago. Then she looked over her shoulder at Mum, giving her a wink. Mum looked appalled.

'Oh God! She's matchmaking again!' Mum whispered. 'What is she *like*?' She saw I was looking anxious. 'Don't worry, Em, if this place of his looks out of our league we'll just say we don't fancy it. I've been thinking, I'd rather like to get

200

fish and chips and eat them on the beach. Wouldn't that be fun?'

I knew Mum was just saying that because she was worried this fat man's recommended restaurant was going to be too expensive. But it turned out to be the perfect place, a small friendly very cheap restaurant crammed with local families. They were sitting on wooden benches, with red candles on the trestle tables and red-and-white place mats. A red-cheeked lady in a red-and-white checked apron greeted us as if we were long-lost relatives. She made Vita twirl round to show off her outfit, she tickled Maxie under the chin, and she stroked my long hair. She said in Spanish that she   thought my hair was beautiful, definitely my crowning glory. The fat man translated for me.

'Don't you wish we could speak fluent Spanish, Julie?' said Gran. She gave the fat man a big lipsticky smile. 'You're so clever. I don't suppose you could translate the menu for us too? In fact, why don't you join us for supper? We'd love that, wouldn't we, Julie?'

'Mum!' my mum hissed.

'Now then, don't look so embarrassed. He can always say no,' said Gran.

'But I'm going to say yes please!' he said. 'I'm Eddie, by the way.'

'I'm Ellen and this is Julie, my daughter. She's separated, on her own now. Julie, make room for Eddie. Em, mind out the way. Come and sit beside me.'

I glared at Gran. I didn't want to be stuck sitting beside her. I didn't want this Eddie muscling in on *my* special meal for Mum. I sighed meaningfully and started heaving myself up off my chair.

'No, no, Em, you stay where you are. I'll sit next to your gran,' said Eddie, settling himself. 'So, Ellen, are you single now too?'

'Oh yes, I'm definitely single,' said Gran.

'I'm single too,' Vita announced, knowing it would make them all chuckle. 'I used to have this boyfriend Charlie right from when we started in Reception, but he wouldn't play in the little house with me so I chucked him, and then in Year One I had two boyfriends, Paul and Mikey, and they kept fighting each other and they wouldn't stop even though I kept telling them off, so I chucked them both and then . . .' She went on and on and on. Eddie laughed obligingly, and then turned to me.

'What about you, Em? Have you led a checkered love-life too?'

'Em doesn't like boys, she just likes her boring old books,' said Vita, sighing at her sad sister.

'I'm a total bookworm myself,' said Eddie. 'So what do you like to read then, Em?'

'I'm really into Jenna Williams,' I said.

'What sort of books does she write?' Eddie asked, unbelievably. He'd never ever heard of Jenna Williams!

Before I had a chance to tell him all about her, Gran jumped in again.

'Our Julie's a great reader too, always got her head in a book,' she said. 'Isn't that right, Julie? She reads all sorts, even classics.'

'I don't, Mum! I just had a go at *Pride and Prejudice* once, after it had been on the telly.'

'She's so modest, my Julie. She was bright at school, could have gone on to university, but— well—she had other plans,' said Gran, shaking her head at me.

'I didn't go to university myself. Left school at sixteen, did an apprenticeship, worked my way up the building trade, got my own business, did very nicely, thank you, then when the kids were off our hands I sold off the business and planned to sun myself in Spain and live happily ever after.' Eddie shook his head sadly. 'But then my wife got ill, and it didn't work out the way we wanted.'

'How sad. Still, you never know what might be in the cards for the future,' said Gran. She smiled at him and passed him the menu. 'Right, Eddie, we're in your hands. What shall we eat?'

I glared at Gran again. I'd wanted to show Mum the menu and tell her to choose whatever she fancied. Gran and this Eddie seemed to have taken over completely. Eddie felt we should sample a proper paella, all of us sharing. Gran said she thought this was a splendid idea, though she looked a little taken aback when this huge sizzling plateful arrived and she saw it was seafood and rice. It smelled marvellous but we all wondered if there were tentacles and slimy fishy bits hidden in its depths.

'Fantastic!' Gran said determinedly.

Vita and Maxie weren't convinced.

'I don't like it,' said Vita. 'Can't I have chips?'

'Chips!' said Maxie.

'Now don't play up, you two,' said Mum.

'Oh, let them have chips, if that's what they want!' said Gran, unbelievably. 'Anything to keep them quiet!'

'What about you, Em? Would you like some paella?' Mum asked. Underneath the table she reached for my hand and gave it a quick squeeze.

I ended up having a big plateful of paella *and* a huge portion of chips, and they were both delicious.

'I like to see a child with a healthy appetite,' said Eddie.

'That's our Em,' said Gran, not breathing a word about my diet.

I decided to make the most of things and ordered a big ice cream for pudding. So did Eddie. Vita and Maxie clamoured for ice cream too, but Mum asked the waitress if they could share one on two plates. Mum didn't want an ice cream herself, or any other kind of pudding, though I tried hard to persuade her.

'Surely you're not on a diet, Julie, there's nothing of you,' said Eddie.

'She's lost a little weight because life's been a bit of a struggle for her recently,' said Gran. 'But things are looking up now, aren't they, dear? Though she does work ever so hard. She runs her own hairdressing business—she's so enterprising. Tell Eddie all about the Good Fairy business, Julie.'

'Oh Mum, give it a rest!' said my mum.

Eddie excused himself tactfully and went off to the gents.

'Isn't he *gorgeous*!' said Gran, leaning forward, showing quite a lot of her chest above her pink lacy top. 'Julie, for pity's sake, *talk* more, try to impress him. He's obviously very smitten but you've got to encourage him.'

'I don't want to,' said Mum. 'I keep telling you, I'm not interested in any other men. And he's old, anyway.'

'He's *mature*. That's what you need, a real man

who wants to settle down, not some boyish fool who'll play around and break your heart. Eddie's still in his prime.'

'And he's fat.'

'He's just well built, and he obviously likes his food. He looks a fine figure of a man. He wears his clothes well too. His cream trousers are beautifully cut and I love his shirt, don't you? Exactly the colour of his eyes.'

'You're just impressed with him because he's got money,' Mum snapped.

'Well, money's not such a bad thing, is it? Think of the difference he'd make to all our lives! And you would be giving him back a reason for living, companionship, fun, laughter. He even gets on well with the kids, so he'd be a good father to them.'

'We've *got* a father,' I said indignantly. 'Stop it, Gran. You're spoiling everything. This is meant to be *our* meal, me treating Mum and you lot. Now it looks like I've got to fork out for this Eddie too.'

'Of course you haven't, Em,' said Gran. 'As a matter of fact, I think Eddie's over there sorting out the bill himself.'

I could have burst into tears. I wanted to rush over, elbow Eddie out the way and pay myself, but Mum hung onto me.

'We'll have *your* meal tomorrow, Em,' she said quickly.

'I think Eddie might have other plans,' Gran said. 'Maybe he'll want to invite you out for a quiet meal, just the two of you. Don't worry, I'll babysit the kids. You just go for it, Julie.'

'I don't *want* to go for him, Mum! And you're wrong too, I don't think he fancies me in the slightest,' said Mum.

But after we'd all finished thanking him for the lovely meal (I said it through gritted teeth) Eddie said how very much he'd enjoyed meeting us all—and that he hoped we could all meet up again before the end of our holiday.

'What about tomorrow evening?' Gran said quickly.

'Well, that would be great,' said Eddie. 'But I was actually wondering about a quieter meal for two tomorrow?'

Gran grinned triumphantly. Mum went bright red. She looked at Eddie, agonized. But he wasn't looking at her.

He was looking at Gran.

'Would you care to come out with me tomorrow, Ellen?' he said.

Twelve

I couldn't wait to go back to school to see Jenny and Yvonne.

'You'll never guess what happened!' I said.

'Your dad came back and you all went on holiday together?' said Jenny.

I swallowed. 'As if!'

'Yeah, tell me about it,' said Yvonne. 'Mind you, I'm not sure I'd *want* mine back. He kept moaning he was tired because my new little half sister keeps crying at night. He'd only come down the swirly chute and swim in the proper pool once. Most of the time we had to stay in the boring little toddler's pool with boring little Bethany.'

'I went swimming heaps of times. I can swim freestyle now—*and* dive.'

'You can do a proper dive?' said Yvonne. 'You mean just off the side?'

'And off the springboard!'

'Hey, will you teach me?'

'Sure,' I said airily. 'Let's go swimming together. You too, Jen.'

'No, catch me, I *hate* getting my head under the

209

water. I didn't go in swimming properly all holiday, I just paddled. I suppose I'm a bit of a wimp.'

'But you've got beautifully brown,' I said. 'Honestly, Gran kept smothering me in so much sunscreen you wouldn't ever think I'd had a week in Spain. Listen, let me tell you about Gran! She's got a boyfriend!'

'She's what? But she's old!' said Yvonne.

'And she's all grumpy and bossy, if you don't mind my saying so, Em,' said Jenny.

'It's true, though! Isn't it amazing! He's five years younger than her too, so Mum and I keep kidding her that Eddie is her toy boy. You think she'd get mad but she just goes all pink and giggly. She isn't anywhere *near* as grumpy and bossy now.'

'Does she see a lot of him?' asked Jenny.

'Well, he lives in Spain, but she went out with him while she was there, and now she's home she keeps phoning. He's coming over sometime this autumn and then she's planning to stay with him sometime in the winter,' I said.

'Have you seen them snogging?' Yvonne asked, giggling.

'People their age don't *snog*!' said Jenny.

'Oh yes they do!' I said. 'You should have seen them saying goodbye at the airport! Vita and Maxie kept going yuck-yuck-yuck—you know what little kids are like—but Gran and Eddie took no notice, going slurpy slurpy like film stars.'

'Do you think they'll get *married*?' said Jenny. 'That would be cool, then you'd get to be a bridesmaid.'

'Oh ha ha, imagine me in a bridesmaid's pink satin frock. I'd look like a giant meringue,' I said.

'You can have any colour bridesmaid's dress.

Blue would suit you, Em. Or green.'

'OK. Think blue whale. Think jolly green giant,' I said.

'What are you on about?' said Yvonne. 'Are you fussed because you're fat?'

'You don't call people *fat*, Yvonne, it's rude. You say big or large or overweight,' said Jenny. Then she put her arm round me. 'But actually, Em, you're not *as* big as you used to be.'

'Yeah, I thought you looked a bit different,' said Yvonne. She pinged the waistband of my school skirt. 'Look, it's not tight any more. Maybe it was just puppy fat before. Or puppy *big*!'

'Woof woof!' I said, clowning about like a big puppy, making them both laugh.

I really was losing weight, even though I didn't always stick totally to any boring old diet. I just didn't fill up all the time on chocolate.

I started to go swimming regularly too. I went with Yvonne on Saturday and we had a great time. She was just as fast as me at breaststroke but I could beat her at freestyle! I taught her to dive too, though we couldn't practise much as the pool attendant said diving wasn't really allowed during public swimming sessions.

'You could join our special Earlybirds club though, and come and train before school if you wanted.'

Yvonne wasn't keen because it would mean having to get up way too early. I wondered if I wanted to go by myself. It was so great to be good at something like swimming. I got such a thrill storming past heaps of other kids in the water. I was so used to being rubbish in any race and coming last. I wondered if I could ever come *first* in

211

a swimming race if I trained hard.

I asked Mum if I could join this Earlybirds club.

'Oh Em, it's such a rush in the morning as it is. I honestly don't see how I could manage taking you all the way to the baths and getting Vita and Maxie ready for school and me off to my first hairdressing appointment.'

'I could take myself there, Mum, you know I could!'

'Well, I know you're more grown up than any of us, but I'm sure they wouldn't allow it.' Mum paused. 'Well, we'll find out.'

There was a notice up in the swimming baths. CHILDREN UNDER NINE YEARS OLD MUST BE ACCOMPANIED BY AN ADULT.

'It's OK, Mum! I'm over nine! I can go!' I said triumphantly.

Mum still took me the first time, while Gran took Vita and Maxie to school.

I started to get nervous as we got nearer the baths. My tummy was in a knot by the time I got in the changing rooms. I could see a whole bunch of kids under the showers. They were all much much much thinner than me. The girls all had sleek black costumes too, real serious swimmer stuff. No one else had a big blue flowery costume. I pulled it right down at the back to make sure it covered my bottom. I held in my stomach, so that the knot tightened.

Mum walked with me to the edge of the pool. There were lots of children swimming. They threshed up and down, up and down, in lane after lane. They were all so fast, so fit, so fantastic. They could all swim much much much better than me.

'I want to get out of here!' I mumbled to Mum.

I was all set to scoot straight back into the cubicle, pull my clothes on and make a run for it. But a big blonde woman in a tracksuit spotted me and came bounding over in her bouncy trainers. She beamed at me cheerily. She was surprisingly fat herself, filling her tracksuit right up so that it clung as snugly as a wetsuit.

'Hello there, chickie. I'm Maggie. Have you come for the Earlybirds session? Let's see what you can do.'

'I'm not good enough,' I said, looking at the children splashing up and down the pool. 'I can't swim as fast as that.'

'Don't worry, neither can I, not nowadays!' said Maggie. 'Come on, jump in and show me.'

I looked round at Mum. She gave me a little thumbs-up sign.

I jumped in the water. I was in such a nervous state I kept my mouth open and swallowed a bucketful. I coughed and choked, going scarlet.

'Don't worry, darling,' said Maggie. 'Take a few deep breaths, that's the ticket. Now—swim!'

I swam while she watched. Then she nodded.

'I'm not as good as the others, am I?' I said.

'Not yet. But you've got potential. You wait and see. You stick at it, and you'll be swimming like a little fish by Christmas, and maybe you'll be the star of all my Earlybirds by next summer.'

I wasn't so sure, but I did stick at it. I went most days before school. A few of the prettiest, skinniest girls giggled and whispered when I was in the shower, but I did my best not to take any notice. Some of the boys were OK. I helped one very little boy sort out his locker when his key had jammed and he tagged round after me like I was his mum.

213

He wouldn't give his own mum a look-in, it was all 'I want *Emily* to dry my hair' or 'I want *Emily* to tie my laces.' I ended up having to fuss round him just like I did with Maxie and Vita but I didn't mind. He was quite sweet. He was wicked in the pool, so fast and so strong. I knew I'd never get to be as good as him even though he was half my size. Still, after a few weeks I did get a lot quicker, and could just about beat some of the smaller girls.

'You're going great guns, chickie,' said Maggie. She tweaked my upper arms. 'Getting muscles just like Popeye too! My Emily Earlybird is getting mega fit.'

She was just joking, being sweet to me, but I really did seem to be getting a lot fitter. I was still rubbish at PE and games at school, but at least I didn't get so breathless now. I was really getting thinner too. I was still *fat*, but not ultra-wobbly-enormous.

'You're like Nellie in Jenna Williams's *Teen* series,' said Jenny. 'She goes swimming in *Teens on a Diet*, remember? Hey, Em, did you know Jenna Williams is doing a big book-signing up in London next Saturday?'

'Really!'

'Yes, there was all this stuff on her fan club website. She's got a special new book coming out. It sounds soooo good—*The Emerald Sisters*—and there's a big new bookshop in Covent Garden called Addeyman's. Jenna Williams is going to be there all day. I'm so mad though, because we're going to stay with my gran and grandad in Devon that weekend. I've begged and pleaded with my mum but she says I've got to go with them, there's just no way I can make them see reason, so if I give

214

you all my books, Em, will you get Jenna Williams to sign them?'

I blinked at Jenny, trying to take it all in. 'Next Saturday? Jenna Williams is really going to be there? You can actually meet her and talk to her and get her to sign books?'

'*You* can, you lucky thing. *I* can't. But you will take all my books to be signed, won't you? Please say you will, Em. Then I'll be your best friend for ever.'

'Hey, *I'm* your best friend!' said Yvonne, giving her a nudge.

'Yes, but if you read Jenna Williams like Em and me you'd find out you can have *two* best friends, like in her book *Friends For Ever*, when Emma and Ali are parted but then Emma gets to be friends with Jampot as well. And threesomes work perfectly—look at Nellie and Marnie and Nadia in the *Teen* books.'

'Will you just shut *up* about boring old Jenna Williams and her silly old books,' said Yvonne, yawning hugely. 'Don't you two ever think of anything else?'

I found it very difficult to think about anything else.

I badly wanted to go up to London on Saturday and meet Jenna Williams.

I waited until Mum got home from work, and we were all having tea together. It was Spanish omelette. Gran now had this thing about all things Spanish. We were just waiting for her to scrape her hair into a bun and don a frilly flamenco frock.

'I don't like Spanish omelette. I just want chips,' said Vita.

'I want chips too,' said Maxie.

215

'Stop it,' said Gran. 'Eat your lovely omelette up, Vita, and set your brother a good example.'

'But it's horrible,' said Vita, poking it with her fork. 'Look at all these bits hiding inside!'

'Lovely vegetables,' said Gran.

'Yucky vegetables,' said Vita. 'It looks like someone's been secretly sick inside my omelette.'

'Vita! Stop being so naughty, especially when Gran's been kind enough to cook us all a meal,' Mum said.

'Yucky sicky yucky sicky,' Maxie chanted.

Mum pretended to swat him. She smiled wearily at me. 'Thank God I've got one sensible child. You're ever so quiet, Em. Nothing's wrong, is there?'

'No, everything's fine.'

'How are you doing at swimming?'

'Great. Maggie taught me how to do a racing dive this morning.'

'Are you in a swimming race, Em?' said Gran, scraping Vita's offending vegetables out of her omelette.

'I'm not fast enough to *enter* any races yet, but I'll know how to do the proper dive when I am,' I said.

'Yucky sicky yucky sicky,' Maxie persisted.

'Put another record on, Maxie,' said Mum, rubbing her forehead.

'Sucky yicky sucky yicky,' Maxie chanted, and then screamed with laughter.

'Mum . . .'

'Yes, love?'

'Mum, you know Jenna Williams?'

'Yes. Well?'

'She's doing this big book-signing up in London

on Saturday. I so want to see her, and I've promised Jenny I'll take all her books to get them signed, and I can't let her down because she's my best friend, and anyway, I'm desperate to go myself. Can I go, Mum? Please say yes. Please please please!'

'Oh, Em.' Mum leaned back in her chair, rubbing her forehead again. 'I know how much you'd like to go, pet. But it's Saturday. I can't take you on a Saturday. Especially not this week, I've got a big wedding. I have to be at the bride's house at breakfast time, and I'll be working flat out till I start at the Palace. Then I can't let Violet down, it's just the two of us now, and there's a whole disco-dancing troupe coming in to get their hair dyed violet for their Deep Purple routine.'

'I know, Mum. But you don't need to take me. I can go by myself.'

'Don't be silly, Em,' said Gran.

'I'm *not* silly! Look, I go swimming by myself, don't I, and I manage perfectly, and then I go to school by myself, I do heaps and heaps of stuff by myself, so I'll be fine going to London, it's just a simple train ride, and I promise I won't talk to any strangers. Please say yes, Mum.'

'You *are* being silly, love,' Mum said despairingly. 'I couldn't possibly let you go up to London by yourself.'

'But I have to meet Jenna Williams, Mum, I just have to!'

'Oh Em, don't.' Mum pushed her plate away and buried her head in her hands. 'If only your dad was here to take you!'

She whispered it, but we all heard.

Maxie stopped chanting his stupid nonsense and

slid under the table. Vita reached for Dancer and put her thumb in her mouth. I clasped my hands so tightly my emerald ring bit hard into my finger.

'We don't need him,' said Gran. 'I'll take Em.'

We stared at her.

'Don't look so gob-smacked!' she said. 'Why shouldn't I take my grand-daughter to meet this Jenna Williams? I know she means a lot to her. So I'll take her.'

'Oh Gran!' I said, and I rushed round the table and gave her a big hug.

'Hey, hey, get off me, you daft banana, you're squashing me,' said Gran, but she gave me a quick hug back.

'But Mum, what about Vita and Maxie? I can't take them with me, not if I've got all the bridal hairdos and then all the purple tints at the Palace.'

'Oh well, in for a penny, in for a pound,' said Gran. 'I'll look after them too. We'll have a proper treat day out in London.'

'But we don't like Jenna Williams,' said Vita. 'She's not a treat for me and she's certainly not a treat for Maxie because he can't even read yet.'

'You'll have to choose your treat too,' said Gran.

'Oh wow!' said Vita. 'Then I want to go to a ballet and I want to go to a rock concert and I want to go to a big big shop and buy heaps of clothes and toys and my own television and I want to go to the zoo and ride on an elephant and feed the tigers and—'

'I'll feed *you* to the tigers, you greedy little madam,' said Gran, laughing. 'What about you, Maxie? What do you want for your treat?'

'Want to go on the helter-skelter,' said Maxie.

'The what?' said Gran. 'Oh great! Where do you

think I'm going to find a helter-skelter? In the middle of Piccadilly Circus?'

'Not the circus, I don't like the clowns,' said Maxie. He looked surprised when we all laughed at him.

'I'm going to be the clown, taking you three up to London,' said Gran, sighing. 'I'm beginning to regret I ever made the offer.'

I gasped, wondering if she might go back on it altogether. She saw my face.

'Don't worry, Em. I *will* take you. You deserve a little treat.'

I fixed up my towel nest in the bath that night and did a little rewriting of my Dancer story. I tore out several pages about Dancer's mean ancient grandma reindeer who had cross-eyes and knobbly knees and a habit of giving her grandchildren a sharp thwack about the head with her gnarled antlers.

'Em? Are you writing in there?' Mum called. She slipped into the bathroom and sat on the edge of the bath. 'How's it going? Let's have a peep.'

I showed her my discarded pages. They made Mum giggle.

'I should stick them back in, they're very funny,' she said. 'You know what, Em. I should take your story with you on Saturday and show Jenna Williams.'

'Really? No, she'd think it was rubbish. It *is* rubbish, all babyish and stupid.'

'I think it's really great. Just show it to her, Em. I'm sure she'd be tickled that you like writing stories too.'

'I can't believe Gran's actually taking me! Why is she suddenly being nice to me?'

'Oh Em, work it out! If it hadn't been for you she'd never have met her Eddie. Isn't it a laugh, those two. She's so head over heels, just like a teenager. And yet she's always been so anti men. She couldn't stick my dad.'

'Or mine,' I said. I paused. 'Mum, don't you really want to meet anyone else?'

Mum reached out and twiddled with a long strand of my hair. 'I really don't, Em. I can't get interested. Not even if Robbie Williams and David Beckham came along and had a fight over who was taking me out tonight.'

'You just want Dad back?' I whispered.

'I don't even know if I *really* want Dad back either,' said Mum. 'But anyway, that's not going to happen. No matter how many times you mutter it under your breath!'

I muttered it anyway in bed afterwards, Dancer on my hand and my story clasped to my chest. I couldn't decide whether to show Jenna Williams or not. I planned in my head what I was going to wear to see her on Saturday. It had to be my green dress and my emerald ring, seeing as her new book was called *The Emerald Sisters*. My new denim jacket would detract from the all-green theme, but I could take it off inside the shop. I could ask Mum to do my hair for me, tying it with the green ribbon.

Then I had an even better idea. I couldn't wait till the morning. I slid out of bed and pattered along the landing to Mum's room. She was sitting up in bed reading a book called *How to Enjoy Being Newly Single*.

'Em? What is it, love?'

'Mum, will you dye my hair?'

'What? No, you know I won't! Not till you're

sixteen.'

'I don't want it dyed *permanently*. I just want it tinted emerald-green for Saturday! Oh please, please, please, Mum, it would look so cool and I know Jenna Williams would love it.'

'I'm not sure even your newly constructed nice gran would take a bright green grand-daughter up to London,' said Mum.

In the end she got up very early on Saturday morning and sprayed me one small emerald streak down my fringe. It looked sooo cool.

Vita wanted one too. And Maxie.

'No, this is just for Em. She's the one who's Princess Emerald after all,' said Mum. 'Now I want you all to be very very good for Gran, do you hear me? Don't give her any cheek, Em. Don't show off, Vita. And don't throw one of your wobblies, Maxie.'

Mum kissed us all goodbye and went off to blow-dry the bride and all her bridesmaids. I poured out cornflakes for Vita and Maxie and then made a round of toast and a pot of tea for Gran. I set it all out on a tray as prettily as possible, even cutting off the crusts and dividing the marmalade toast into neat triangles. It glowed against the best blue-and-white china. I cut one orange flower off her potted chrysanthemum and floated it in a little glass dish. Then I carried it carefully to Gran's bedroom.

She was still asleep, looking so much softer without all her make-up. She had a little smile on her face. Perhaps she was dreaming about Eddie.

She frowned when she woke up and saw her special breakfast tray. 'Why on earth have you used my willow pattern, Em? I don't want to risk getting it chipped. And you're not supposed to pick the

221

flowers off pot plants, you silly girl.'

'I just wanted to make your breakfast look nice for you, Gran,' I said.

Gran sat up properly, smoothing her hair with her fingers. Her face smoothed out too. 'Oh, Em. Well. It *does* look nice. Almost too good to eat. Thank you, dear.' Then she blinked. 'Em? What's happened to your *hair*?'

She wasn't at all pleased about the green streak, but there was nothing she could do about it.

'Jenna Williams will like it,' I said.

'Then Jenna Williams has no taste,' said Gran. 'It's criminal to muck about dyeing your lovely hair.'

'My crowning glory! *Eddie* said so,' I said, bouncing on Gran's bed.

'Watch my tea! Keep still, Em.'

'I can't, I'm so excited! I'm going to see Jenna Williams!'

'All this fuss! You're a weird kid, our Em,' said Gran. 'Still, it's good to see you so full of beans.'

We had a little argument when we were about to leave home.

'What on earth are those huge great carrier bags?' Gran asked.

'It's all Jenny's Jenna Williams books. I promised I'd get them signed for her. Then there's *my* Jenna Williams books too,' I said. There was also my Dancer story, but I felt too shy to tell Gran that I might be going to show it to Jenna Williams. I had Dancer too, but I didn't have to carry her— she sat on my hand and helped me carry the bags.

'For pity's sake, you can't lump all that lot round London. Jenny can get her own books signed,' said Gran.

'But she *can't*, Gran, that's the whole point. I *promised*. I can't let her down, she's my friend. And I've got to get *my* books done.'

'Choose one of your books and one of Jenny's, that's more than enough. And for pity's sake take that silly puppet off, we're certainly not carting that up to London too.'

'Dancer's part of our family, Gran!'

'Don't talk so wet! She's not yours anyway, she's Vita's.'

I had done a deal with Vita (involving a big bag of fizzy cola sweets, my silver glitter nail varnish and my purple gel pen) that I got to wear Dancer. I needed to hide my emerald ring so that Gran wouldn't fuss about me losing it. I also needed Dancer's comfort and support in case I was struck dumb in front of Jenna Williams.

'I don't mind sharing Dancer with Em,' Vita said sweetly, in a goody-goody little girly lisp.

Gran patted Vita and shook her head at me. 'All right, Em, if you want to look a fool wearing that reindeer puppet, then so be it. But you really *can't* drag all those books along. I can't carry them for you, you know how my hands play me up. You'll end up with arthritis too, lumping heavy bags around like that.'

'OK, OK, I won't take the carrier bags,' I said, changing tactics. 'I'll just take a *few* books, and I'll put them in my school bag and carry them on my back.'

I rushed off to the bedroom. I managed to cram nearly *all* Jenny's and my books into my school bag, with my Dancer story squashed in at the side. I nearly fell flat on my face when I dragged the bag onto my back, but I was sure I'd get used to the

223

weight. I pretended it was feather-light in front of Gran, and thank goodness she didn't see just how bulky the bag had become.

I was boiling hot and exhausted by the time we'd walked ten minutes to the railway station, and my long hair kept getting stuck under the bag straps so that I nearly got scalped if I bent my head.

'Are you all right, Em? Is that bag too heavy for you?' said Gran.

'I'm fine! It's not heavy at all,' I said determinedly.

It was an enormous relief to take the bag off on the train. I wriggled my sore shoulders. Vita and Maxie copied me, and we made up our own mad little sitting-down dance routine, left shoulder wriggle, right shoulder wriggle, left arm out, right arm out, hands on top of head, both hands waving in the air, repeat as often as you like.

We repeated it a great many times. Gran told us off at first, saying we were making an exhibition of ourselves, but some other children started copying us, and then their mum and dad joined in too. Gran raised her eyebrows and sighed at all of us— but she had one quick little go herself as the train drew into Waterloo Station.

'I looked up the Jenna Williams website on the computer at work,' Gran said. 'She's not signing until one o'clock, so we've got plenty of time to look around first.'

We walked along the embankment, staring up at the great Millennium Wheel.

'Oh, Gran, can we go up in it?' said Vita.

'There's a big queue already. I don't think so, pet. I can't stand hanging around in queues. It makes my back ache just standing still—and it's such a waste of time,' said Gran.

'Oh please please please, pretty please, Gran,' said Vita.

'Well . . .' said Gran, wavering.

Maxie stared at them as if they'd gone mad. 'No!' he said. 'No, it's too big, too high, too scary!'

'I thought you liked helter-skelters,' said Gran. 'They're big and high and scary.'

'I'm on a mat on someone's lap in a helter-skelter,' said Maxie.

'Tell you what, Maxie, we could put my jacket on the floor of the glass pod and you could sit on my lap and then you'd feel safe as safe,' I said.

We persuaded him it would work. We had to queue for tickets and then we had to join another queue to get on the wheel.

'My blooming back!' said Gran. 'I don't know about Maxie sitting down, but I'm going to have to *lie* down, stretched full out. I don't think this is a very good idea.'

Maybe Gran was right. I kept remembering a Jenna Williams story called *Flora Rose*, where little Lenny gets terribly scared on the Millennium Wheel. I was starting to get a little bit anxious myself. It did look very very high, and you were shut up in the pod a long time. What would happen if the wheel got stuck when you were right at the top, unable to get out?

'I don't want to!' Maxie whined. 'It's scary.'

'No, it's not,' I lied. I tried to pick him up but I couldn't manage to carry him *and* the book bag.

Gran had to carry Maxie, though she sighed some more when his dusty shoes kicked at her pale pink skirt.

'Watch your feet, Maxie! And stop that whining,

it's getting on my nerves.'

Maxie stopped whining and started full-bodied sobbing.

'Oh, for pity's sake!' said Gran. 'Look, this is meant to be a treat. Do stop acting as if I'm torturing you. Maybe we're just going to have to give up on this, Em.'

'No, no, *please* let's go on, I want to, don't be mean!' Vita wailed. She started sobbing too.

'Oh, dear God, stop it, both of you, or I'll knock your heads together. Why did I ever say I'd do this?' said Gran, looking at me balefully.

'You said you'd take us up to London because you're a lovely kind gran and I'm very very grateful,' I said, laying it on with a trowel—no, a huge great *spade* of praise!

'Yes, I am lovely and kind—and very very stupid,' said Gran, hanging onto Maxie and Vita. They were trying hard to outsob each other. Gran give them a little shake. They sobbed harder. People were staring.

'Stop it! Stop it at once, you're showing me up! If you don't stop this minute we'll go straight back home without any treats at all,' Gran threatened.

I panicked. 'It's OK, Gran. I'll stay on the ground with Maxie. You go on the wheel with Vita.'

Gran thought about it. 'But then you'll miss out altogether, Em, and you're the only one behaving sensibly. Won't you mind terribly if you don't get to go on the wheel?'

I didn't mind one little bit, but I didn't let on. 'Perhaps I'll get to go on the wheel another time,' I said, trying to look wistful.

'You're a good girl, Em. Here!' Gran fished in her handbag and tucked a five-pound note in my

226

hand. 'Buy yourselves an ice cream while you're waiting for Vita and me.'

I was more than ready for something to eat. I'd been so busy fixing everyone else's breakfast I'd forgotten to eat any myself. I bought Maxie and me large 99s from a Whippy ice-cream van. Maxie had given himself hiccups after all that sobbing.

'Lick your ice cream slowly, don't make your hiccups worse,' I said. 'Look, Vita and Gran are getting into their pod. Up they go!'

Maxie shuddered. 'I'm sorry I'm not a big brave boy,' he said forlornly.

'You can't help it, Maxie. Don't worry. What would you like to do for *your* treat then? Vita's had the ride on the wheel. There she is, waving, way up high already, look!'

Maxie ducked his head. 'Don't want to look!' he said.

I waved back to Vita. I picked Maxie's limp arm up and waggled it, so that he was waving too. His other arm waggled in sympathy and he dropped his ice cream on the ground.

'Oh, my ice cream!'

'Oh dear. Well. You can finish mine if you like. Or I'll get you another one. Gran's given me heaps of money.'

'Will that be my treat, another ice cream?' said Maxie.

'No, no, you can choose something else.'

'A helter-skelter?'

'Maxie! Look, there *aren't* any helter-skelters in London, trust me. They're just at funfairs and the seaside. And even if we took you all the way back to the one on the pier, I don't think you'd really like it. You could sit on my lap on the mat, but it's

227

not me you want, is it? It's Dad.'

Maxie put his sticky hands over his ears but I knew he could still hear me.

'I miss him too, Maxie. So much. I'd give anything for him to come back. I've wished it over and over.' I took Dancer off my hand and looked at my ring. 'We could make another wish if you like, on my magic emerald.'

'Will it come true?' said Maxie, taking his hands away from his head.

'Well, it hasn't come true *yet*. But it could come true this time. Shall we try?'

Maxie clasped my hand and we wished for Dad. I muttered a whole lot of stuff. Maxie just went, *'Dad Dad Dad Dad Dad.'* Then we both looked round over our shoulders. There were dads everywhere, shouting, laughing, calling, chatting, joking, pulling funny faces. But not *our* dad.

Dancer wriggled onto my hand and stroked Maxie's cheek with her paw. He brushed her away, not in the mood for her stories. I wasn't really either. I undid my school bag and read the first page of my Dancer book. My heart started thumping. It seemed so stupid now, so totally babyish. Why on earth would Jenna Williams want to read it? She'd probably say something nice to me, but privately she'd be thinking me a totally sad idiot. I crammed my story back into my school bag, hiding it under all the books.

We sat silently on some steps, waiting. It seemed an age before Gran and Vita got out their pod and came over to us. Vita was dancing, twirling round and round. 'It was so great up on the wheel! I saw Buckingham Palace and the Queen waved to me,' she carolled in a cutesie-pie voice.

228

'It was amazing, you could see for miles,' said Gran, jigging around, almost breaking into a dance herself. 'Oh dear, you two, what glum faces! Maxie, you're such a prize banana. Come on then, let's go for a little walk along the embankment.'

'Hadn't we better go and find the bookshop now?' I said anxiously.

'Don't be silly, Em, your blessed Jenna Williams isn't going to be there for an hour and a half. We don't want to be hanging around waiting with nothing to do. No, I want to show you the Globe Theatre—it's only a couple of minutes away, we could see it from the pod. It's been built just like a proper Elizabethan theatre.'

'I want to go on the stage and dance!' said Vita, holding out her arms and simpering, as if she could hear tumultuous applause.

So we trudged along the embankment. My book bag got heavier and heavier and heavier, but I didn't dare complain. Maxie trailed beside me, scuffing his feet. Vita stopped prancing and started pestering for an ice cream, because Maxie and I had already had one. Gran had to stand on one foot and adjust the straps on her sandals, sighing.

'Maybe this isn't such a good idea,' she said. 'It looked so near when we were in the pod, but it's obviously miles away.'

'Miles and miles and miles,' Maxie said glumly.

'It's not fair, *I* want an ice cream,' said Vita.

'What's the time? Maybe we should start going back now,' I said. 'I want to be first in the queue at Addeymans bookshop.'

'I told you, there's heaps of time yet. We'll just go as far as that big chimney, see it? I think that's Tate Modern, the art gallery. I wouldn't mind getting some postcards,' said Gran.

'To send to Eddie?' I said.

'Maybe,' said Gran. 'Though I don't want to send any picture of daft scribble or dead cows or what have you.'

We didn't get to go inside the gallery. We all stared transfixed at the huge sculptures outside, on the forecourt. There were four gigantic towers, one red, one yellow, one blue and one green, with shiny silver slides spiralling round and round, down to the ground. There were doors at the bottom, and stairs leading up inside.

'Helter-skelters!' Maxie shrieked.

'Well I never! There you are, Maxie, your wish come true! They *look* like helter-skelters, certainly,' said Gran. 'But they're not real ones.'

'They look real. I want to go on the red one!' said Vita.

'You can't go *on* them, they're sculptures,' said Gran.

'No, Gran, look, people *are* going on them,' I said, pointing to heads bobbing at the top of each tower.

'So they are! Well, all right, I don't see why you can't go too,' said Gran. 'Maxie, you go on with Em.'

'No, not Em. I'm going with *Dad*!' said Maxie.

'Your dad's not here, Maxie,' said Gran, sighing.

'He will be, he will be! We wished it, and it's come true, it really has!' said Maxie, his face radiant.

'Oh Maxie,' I said, but I wondered if Dad *might* just be up at the top of these magical helter-skelters, waiting for us.

I took Maxie and Vita on all four helter-skelters. They weren't dark inside. They were lit up with a wonderful golden glow and there were pictures to look at as we climbed the steps. There were strawberries and scarlet ribbons, roses and Little Red Riding Hood in the red helter-skelter; bananas and teddy bears, sandpits and smiley suns in the yellow helter-skelter; turquoise pools and clear skies, cornflowers and little boy babies in the blue helter-skelter; Granny Smith apples and grassy meadows and an entire Emerald City of Oz in the green helter-skelter.

Everyone emerged at the top with great smiles on their faces before they spiralled all the way downwards on the shiny silver slide.

Everyone but Maxie.

We went up the red helter-skelter, the yellow helter-skelter, the blue helter-skelter, the green helter-skelter. Maxie didn't give the pictures a second glance. He was peering round, looking desperately.

'I give up!' said Gran, when he started sobbing. 'He asks for a helter-skelter in the middle of London. One, two, three, four helter-skelters appear as if by magic. And is this child delighted? No, he bawls his blooming head off!'

'It's not really Maxie's fault, Gran. He was hoping to see . . . someone,' I said. I picked Maxie up and gave him a cuddle, though I could barely move for the big book bag on my back.

I was starting to get a bit anxious. It was twenty to one. I didn't want to be late for Jenna Williams.

I struggled with Maxie for a minute or so.

'Oh, for pity's sake, Em, put him down. Why should you have to lug him along like that?' said Gran. 'Maxie, stop that silly snivelling. Stand on your own two feet and walk properly.'

Maxie couldn't manage it. In the end Gran sighed deeply and took him from me.

'I'll carry you for one minute, that's all. You watch your feet on my skirt, and for pity's sake don't wipe your snotty little face all round my shoulders! Oh, the joys of being a grandma!' said Gran.

We trudged back along the embankment and up over Waterloo Bridge. Gran threatened to chuck Maxie over the parapet into the water. Maxie knew she was joking, but decided to clamber down from her arms and walk under his own steam, just in case.

Vita was the one whining and dragging her feet now, complaining that no one ever carried *her*. I was feeling pretty exhausted myself. I seemed to be carrying at least a hundred Jenna Williams hardbacks in my bag. There was a cold wind up on the bridge but I was so hot my green dress was sticking to me.

'Is it far now, Gran?' I asked.

'Just at the end of the bridge, over the road and round to the left,' said Gran. 'Five minutes. Don't fuss, Em. We'll be there on time. You'll be one of the first to see her. Then we'll all go off and have a bite to eat. I can't wait to sit down, these flipping sandals are killing me. And my back's playing up worse than ever after hauling ten-ton Maxie all over London. I must be mad.'

We got to the end of the bridge. We could see a huge queue winding halfway down the Strand.

'Why are all those people there, Gran?' said Vita.

'Don't ask me,' said Gran. 'Hang on, there's that

musical, *The Lion King*, on at the theatre up ahead. Maybe they're queuing for a show. There's lots of children, that must be it.'

My heart was starting to thump hard inside my green dress. There were lots and lots and lots of children. The girls all seemed to be clutching Jenna Williams books.

We got to the top of the street. The queue was thicker now, ringing round the Covent Garden piazza. There were crash barriers stretching all the way to the big Addeyman's bookshop over at the other side. The queue disappeared inside the door.

There was a huge book display in the window, and emerald fairy lights and a big poster of Jenna Williams and a special notice. JENNA WILLIAMS SIGNING STARTS AT 1 TODAY!

'Oh no!' said Gran. 'I don't believe it! This can't be the Jenna Williams queue!'

'I think it is, Gran,' I said. 'Shall we go back and join on the end?'

'For pity's sake, we can't hang around here all day, Em! We'll be hours and hours!' said Gran.

'Please!' I said.

'No. I'm sorry, but this is beyond a joke. We're all exhausted as it is.'

'Oh Gran, please, I've *got* to meet her.'

'She's just some boring middle-aged lady with a funny haircut,' said Gran, peering at the poster. 'What's so special about her? Look, we'll go to another bookshop and I'll buy you a copy of her new book, all right?'

'But it won't be signed! And I so so so badly want to speak to her. Oh Gran, *please*!' I could feel my face screwing up. Hot tears started dribbling down my cheeks.

233

'Now now! Oh dear Lord, it's bad enough Maxie and Vita bawling their heads off. Don't you start, Em. All right, all right. We'll go to the end of the queue. We'll give it an hour or so, see how we go.'

'Oh Gran, thank you, thank you!' I jumped up and down in spite of my huge bag of books.

'Steady on now! You kids. You're all mad. And so am I. Absolutely barking!'

We went all the way back to the end of the queue. There was a big smiley man at the end, with a pretty little girl about Vita's age.

'Hello!' he said. 'Join the queue! Have you brought your camp beds and your picnic?'

'I wish we had!' said Gran. 'Honestly, isn't this ridiculous! We must be mad.'

'Well, we're just fond parents,' said the man, patting his little girl's silky golden hair. 'This is my Molly. What are your three called?'

Gran simpered. 'I'm their gran, not their mum!' she said. 'This is Em, she's the number one Jenna Williams fan. Then this is Vita and this is Maxie—they're not really into the books yet.'

'I am!' said Vita. 'I like the one with all the parties and the presents where the nasty girl wets herself.'

'I like that one too,' said Molly, giggling. 'And I like *Friends For Ever*. I like the funny dog in that one. I love dogs. I've got this little dog called Maisie, she sleeps on my bed at night.'

'*I've* got this great big reindeer, Dancer—she sleeps in my bed,' said Vita, snatching Dancer off my hand and making her shake paws with Molly.

Molly's dad laughed and admired Dancer. Vita made Dancer prance around, and then let Molly have a go.

'Now me, now me,' said Maxie.

'You can have a go any old time,' said Vita.

'No, let him, he's only little,' said Molly kindly. 'Here you are, Maxie, we'll all take it in turns, eh?'

I took my heavy bag off my shoulders and sighed deeply with relief. Vita and Maxie seemed happy talking to Molly. Gran seemed happy chatting to Molly's nice dad. I didn't want to talk to anyone but Jenna Williams.

Thirteen

We queued and we queued and we queued.

One hour went by. Vita and Molly larked around together. Vita showed Molly how to do a little modern dance routine. Maxie tried to copy them, kicking out his stick legs and nearly tripping people up. Gran seized hold of him and told him to behave. Maxie glared, determined to behave *badly*, but Molly's dad quickly distracted him, producing little sandwiches and tiny cakes and apples from his briefcase. He insisted on sharing them with all of us.

Another hour went by. Vita got fed up with working Dancer and ordered me to take a turn. I made Dancer tell them a story. Then another and another. Molly seemed to like them a lot.

'Are these stories from a book, Emily?' Molly's dad asked.

I shook my head shyly, not realizing he'd been listening too.

'You don't mean to say you make them all up yourself?'

'Well . . . my dad made up some of the stories,' I

239

mumbled.

'Yes, he's very good at making up stories,' Gran sniffed. 'He's out of the picture now,' she mouthed to Molly's dad.

'Em's made up heaps of the Dancer stories herself though. She makes up a new one every day,' Vita said, surprisingly.

'Then you're very clever and inventive, Emily. You should write them all down,' said Molly's dad.

'She has! In a special book and she does pictures too, she showed me,' said Maxie.

'You must be very proud of your grand-daughter,' Molly's dad said to Gran.

Gran smiled and put her arm round my shoulders! 'Yes, she's a clever girl, our Em,' she said. 'Here, darling, if I give you my purse can you go to that coffee shop over there—look, on the other side of the piazza—and buy a coffee for Molly's dad and me, and some juice for all the children.'

I set off importantly, threading my way through the crowds watching the street performers. There was a guy juggling on a very elongated unicycle, a conjurer in a top hat, and a girl in a silver dance frock pointing her toe on a little platform. I thought at first she was a statue because her skin and her hair were painted silver too and she was standing stock-still, not moving a muscle. But then a man threw a coin into a saucer on the ground and the silver girl smiled and twirled round once. Another man threw two coins and she did two twirls and then stood still again, toe pointed, back in her statue position.

I wanted to make her twirl myself, but I didn't dare spend any more of Gran's money. I went and

240

bought all the drinks, wondering how on earth I was going to carry everything. Gran wouldn't carry on calling me clever if I spilled scalding coffee everywhere. Luckily the coffee shop gave me a cardboard tray.

A *third* hour passed, much more slowly. The drinks weren't such a good idea. Gran had to take Maxie and Vita off to find a loo on the second floor of the bookshop. I wouldn't have minded going too, but I was scared that if we all left the queue Gran might give up on the whole idea and drag us home.

Molly's pretty mum turned up, with her two big sisters Jess and Phoebe. They'd all been on a clothes shopping trip. They stood with Molly while her dad went off for a little walk to stretch his legs.

'Don't be long, Dad!' Molly said anxiously.

'I'll be back in ten minutes, tops,' he said.

He came back in *exactly* ten minutes, because I counted. Molly didn't bother. She obviously trusted him.

'Dad!' she said, her blue eyes sparkling.

She leaned against him and he clasped his hands loosely round her neck, tickling her under her chin.

I wished I had a dad like that.

I wished wished wished I had a dad who would come back in ten minutes, tops.

I'm sure Vita and Maxie were wishing it too. They'd been so good for so long, but now they started whining and moaning and flinging themselves around.

'It's no good, Em, they can't hang on here much longer,' said Gran. 'I can't either, sweetheart. I'm in agony. I've got to have a sit down soon or I'll just keel over.'

'Oh, Gran. Please let's stay, especially now we've waited all this time. We *can't* give up now! We're nearly in the door.'

There was a kind curly-haired smiley man waiting there, helping everyone get their books open at the right page.

'Have you been waiting for ages?' he said sympathetically to Gran. 'I'm sorry the queue's so long.'

'Well, it's total madness, hanging around like this,' said Gran. 'Still, I suppose it's very good business for your shop.'

'Oh, I don't work for the shop,' he said. 'I'm Bob, Jenna's driver. But I like to help out with the queue if I can.'

'So you know Jenna Williams?' said Molly.

'I certainly do, young lady. Have you got a question you want to ask her?'

'Mmm . . . *I* know, I'm going to ask her if she's got any pets,' said Molly.

'*I'm* going to ask her to put a little girl called Vita in one of her books,' said Vita, smiling cutely.

'Me too. I want her to put a little girl called Maxie in one of her books,' said Maxie, getting muddled.

He went very red when we laughed at him.

'Never mind, Maxie, you're already in the Wild Things book,' I said.

'Are you a Wild Thing, Maxie?' said Bob. 'Oh dear, I hope you're not too scary.' He cowered away from him, pretending to be afraid. Maxie started giggling, delighting in the game.

Then Bob turned to me. 'Is that great big bag full of Jenna Williams books? Goodness, you're obviously a very big fan.'

'She would insist on bringing them all. Some belong to her friends. I told her to leave them behind but Emily wouldn't hear of it,' said Gran.

'What are *you* going to ask Jenna, Emily?' said Bob, helping me pull the books out of my bag.

'I don't know,' I said shyly.

'I think you should ask her to give you a few writing tips,' said Molly's dad. 'Emily's very good at making up stories. She's been keeping the children very happy with her stories while we've been waiting.'

'That's lovely,' said Bob, helping me balance all the opened books in a neat pile. 'There's one more book left in your bag, I think. Here, let me get it out for you.'

'Oh, that's nothing,' I said quickly, trying to stuff the red book back again.

'It's not the reindeer story, is it?' said Molly's dad.

'Well . . . sort of,' I said, embarrassed.

'Can we have a look?'

'Oh no, it's stupid, I don't know why I brought it,' I said.

'Can *I* see?' Molly begged, so I had to let her.

Her mum and dad read bits over her shoulder.

'Oh Emily, it's wonderful! I think you'll be a rival to Jenna Williams when you grow up!' said Molly's mum.

'You'll have to show Jenna Williams,' said Molly's dad.

'No, no, I couldn't!' I said quickly.

'She'd like to see it, I'm sure,' said Bob.

'We're moving again!' said Molly, as the queue surged forward and we were inside the shop at last. It was very hot and very noisy now, with children laughing and chattering and shouting. Some of them had been given balloon animals and they kept making horrible squeaking noises. Every now and then a child clutched one too tightly and the balloon burst with a bang.

'I don't like it here!' Maxie wailed. 'I want to go out!'

'Please, Maxie, try and be good for just a tiny bit longer,' I begged him. 'We're nearly there now.'

'I *am* trying to be good—but I still don't like it!' Maxie said desperately.

'I don't like it either. People keep pushing me and shoving me and I'm hot and I want another drink,' said Vita.

'We're nearly there, I'm sure we are. Hang on just for a bit, please, *please*,' I said.

Then the queue moved forward again and we turned a corner and we *were* nearly there.

'Look!' said Molly's dad, and he picked her up to show her. 'There's Jenna Williams, over there, in the corner.'

I stood on tiptoe, craning my neck.

I saw a big emerald banner with more fairy lights, and a chair and a table with a shimmering green cloth, and there was this small short-haired lady smiling at everyone, signing book after book. She was wearing a top and skirt the exact same shade of green as my own dress! She was wearing a lot of rings. I wondered if any of them were real emeralds.

I took Dancer off my hand and looked at my own ring, twiddling it round and round my finger.

'My goodness, that's a lovely ring,' said Molly's dad.

'It's an emerald,' I said. 'Well, I think it is.'

'A perfect ring to wear today,' said Molly's mum. 'It won't be long now! Are you getting excited, girls?'

Molly was certainly excited, hugging her dad. Her sisters Jess and Phoebe seemed quite excited too. They'd read lots of Jenna Williams books when they were younger, and although they'd passed them all down to Molly now, they'd kept one favourite one each for Jenna to sign.

I clutched my books and Jenny's books, tucked Dancer under my arm and hooked my bag on my shoulder, in a terrible fluster. I wished I'd gone to the loo when I'd had the chance. I tried to sort out a sensible question in my head. I wanted to learn it by heart so I wouldn't make a fool of myself. It was so silly, I'd been longing to meet Jenna Williams all my life, I'd queued for hours and hours to see her . . . and yet now I was starting to feel weirdly scared.

What if I couldn't get my words out properly? What if I just stood there blushing like an idiot? What if I dropped Jenny's books? Oh dear, what was I going to do if Jenna Williams asked my name and then started to write *'To Emily'* in Jenny's books?

The little cluster of children around Jenna Williams suddenly moved away, waving and smiling, and Molly and her mum and dad and sisters went up to the signing desk. They were there a long time. Molly didn't seem a bit shy. She was saying all sorts of things, making Jenna Williams laugh, while her family looked on fondly.

Molly's dad bought a copy of *The Emerald Sisters* for Molly, a copy for Jess and a copy for Phoebe. Molly was really too young for the story and Jess and Phoebe were too old. Then he picked up a fourth copy from the big glossy green pile.

'This one's for you, Emily,' he said. 'Come and get it signed!'

I stumbled, desperately trying not to drop my pile of unwieldy books. Vita dodged round me and got to Jenna Williams first.

'Hi, Jenna, I'm Vita. I just love your books,' she said. 'Will you put a girl called Vita in one of them?'

'I might just do that. Vita's a lovely name,' said Jenna Williams.

'I'm Maxie. My name's already in a book about Wild Things,' said Maxie.

'I know. I like that Wild Thing book,' said Jenna Williams.

Gran was poking me in the back. 'You go and say something, Em!'

I still hung back, agonizingly shy.

'Oh, for pity's sake, don't tell me you've been struck dumb, when we've been queuing all these hours!' said Gran. She shook her head at Jenna Williams. 'Kids! And this one's your number one fan, too!'

Jenna Williams smiled at me. 'Ah, are you Emily, the one who writes reindeer stories?'

Molly's dad grinned at me. I blushed to the roots of my hair.

'Can I see your story for a minute, Emily?' Jenna Williams asked.

She helped me balance all my books and Jenny's books on the table so that I could delve into my bag. I dropped Dancer in the process.

'Oh, is this the reindeer puppet? I hear you've been doing a grand job entertaining the children in the queue. Go on, give me a demonstration.'

I put Dancer on my hand. She had more courage than I did. She didn't mind talking one bit.

'I'm delighted to meet you, Jenna Williams,' she said. 'I'm flattered that you want to look at my story. Here it is.'

She handed her book over to Jenna. She read a little bit, then flicked through the pages.

'It looks wonderful, Emily! It's such a great idea. Watch out, I might put it in one of *my* books!'

'Emily and I would be thrilled if you do!' said Dancer.

'Maybe I'd better write *"To Emily and Dancer"* in your *Emerald Sisters* book,' said Jenna Williams. 'Hey, you're wearing the perfect colour. And I love the matching green streak in your hair!'

'It's in your honour,' said Dancer. 'I wanted my antlers painted emerald-green too.'

'I'm sure they'd have looked very fetching,' said Jenna Williams.

She signed the book that lovely Molly's dad had bought for me, then my paperbacks, and then I managed to ask if she could sign all the hardbacks to Jenny. Her rings flashed and twinkled as she wrote her name over and over again. I looked at the big green ring on her little finger.

'Is that a real emerald?' I whispered.

'Well, I like to pretend it is,' she said. She smiled at me. 'Writers are good at pretending.' She gave me back my Dancer book. 'I think you're definitely going to be a writer yourself one day, Emily. It was lovely meeting you. And Vita and Maxie. And you too, Dancer.'

Dancer waved her paw while I scrabbled with the other hand to get all my signed books back in my bag.

Then Gran took me by the shoulders and steered me away. 'There, happy now? I'm not sure that was worth all that long long wait!' she said.

'Still, how lovely that Jenna thinks Emily will be a writer too,' said Molly's dad.

'You've been very kind to us all,' said Gran. 'Thank Molly's dad for getting you the new book, Em—though we must pay for it.'

'No, no, it's a little gift to you for keeping Molly so happy while we were queuing. And are *you* happy now, Emily? Have all your wishes come true?'

'Almost,' I said. I felt my ring finger through Dancer's fur, turning the emerald again.

'Don't, Em, that tickles!' Dancer nagged. 'Don't waste your time wishing. Don't you ever give up?'

'No, I don't!' I hissed into her small felt ear. 'You shut up for a minute! I'm sick of you hogging the limelight. You're just a glove puppet, OK?'

I shut my eyes and wished one more time.

'Watch where you're going, Emily, it's so crowded,' said Gran, steering me along through the crowded shop. 'Vita? Maxie? For pity's sake, why have you all got your eyes shut?'

'Ssh, Gran, we're all wishing,' said Vita.

'Wishing and wishing and wishing,' said Maxie.

'I give up!' said Gran. 'Now come on, open your eyes this minute and say goodbye to Molly and her family.'

I'd screwed my eyes so tightly shut that everything was blurred for a moment. I blinked, trying to focus, as we pushed our way outside Addeyman's, into the bright daylight. Vita blinked her long lashes as she gave Molly a big hug. Maxie rubbed his eyes and then opened them wide.

He should have kept them shut. The man making the balloon animals was performing for the queue. He was dressed up in baggy white trousers, great big boots and a round red nose.

'A clown!' Maxie shrieked—and started running.

'Oh Lord,' Gran groaned. 'Maxie! Come back here, you little silly! Em, go after him, quick!'

I ran across the piazza after him. Maxie only had little stick legs, but blind panic made him run like the wind.

'Stop, Maxie! Come back! You'll get lost!' I shouted.

Maxie dodged in and out of the crowds, ran even harder away from the juggler on the unicycle—but then stopped dead, staring over at the silver lady.

I rushed up to him. 'Maxie, you're so mad, you *mustn't* run away like that!' I shouted at him.

He didn't blink. He wasn't listening to me. He stood transfixed, eyes huge, pointing at the silver dancing lady.

'She's just a lady pretending to be a statue, Maxie,' I said. 'Come on, back to Gran.'

Maxie was so rigid I couldn't move him. He shook his head wildly and kept pointing. I stared over at the silver lady. Someone had put a whole handful of coins in her plate, so she was twirling round and round while he clapped appreciatively, looking up at her.

He had a scarf round his neck. A knitted scarf all different colurs. A scarf just like the one I knitted Dad last Christmas.

Who was this strange man wearing my dad's scarf? He looked a little like Dad himself, but he was thinner, much more ordinary looking, with boring short black hair sticking straight up.

The man was saying something to the girl. She was trying to get back into her statue pose but he was making her giggle. That was so like Dad.

He put his head on one side, grinning.

It *was* Dad.

'Dad!' I yelled. 'Dad, Dad, Dad!'

I pulled Maxie's arm and we ran full tilt towards him.

'*Dad!*' Maxie shrieked.

He looked round, startled, but he didn't spot us. He said something else to the silver dancer and then started walking away.

'Oh Dad, please, wait, *wait*!' I shouted, running round the piazza, pushing people out the way.

My eyes were fixed on Dad, terrified that he'd disappear.

I forgot all about the unicyclist. I didn't even see him. I careered straight into him, nearly knocking him flying. Maxie tumbled onto his knees, yelling. I staggered too, unbalanced by my huge bag of books. I hurtled forwards, arms out, desperate to catch my dad. I careered straight into him, sending him sideways. I reached out but I couldn't grab him. I fell flat on my face, landing heavily on my arm.

I lifted my head and screamed. '*Dad!*'

'Em! Oh my God, Em!' He was on his knees beside me, clutching me to him, cradling my head.

'Oh Dad, oh Dad, is it really you?' I sobbed. 'Where's your *plait*?'

'Oh darling, never mind my wretched plait. What are you *doing* up in London? Are you all by yourself?'

'I'm here, Dad!' Maxie shouted, limping and

hopping and hurling himself onto Dad.

'My little Maxie! And you look as if you're in the wars too! So where's Vita?'

'I'm here! Oh Daddy, my daddy!' Vita yelled, running too, with Gran right behind her, shoes in her hand, her skirt hitched right up her hips.

'Oh my Lord, it's you, Frankie! I might have known! For pity's sake, what have you done to the kids?' Gran said. 'Maxie, have you hurt yourself?'

'Yes!' said Maxie, clinging to Dad.

'Poor little guy,' said Dad. 'What about you, Em? You went down with such a wallop.'

'My arm hurts,' I said, and I burst into tears.

'I fell over too and *I'm* not crying!' Maxie boasted.

'What's happened to Dancer?' Vita wailed.

I looked at Dancer on the end of my arm. Her antlers were bent and her delicate pink nose was torn right off.

'We'll mend Dancer, Vita, don't worry. But we've got to get Em mended first. Here, let's see what damage you've done.' Dad started gently plucking at Dancer, trying to ease her off. I couldn't help crying harder.

'Stop it, you're obviously hurting her!' Gran said, kneeling down beside us. 'Let me have a look, Em. Don't cry so.'

'I'm fine, really. Dad's not hurting me a bit,' I wept.

Dad rocked me gently, peering at my arm. It was bent at a weird angle. It didn't seem to want to go straight any more.

'I think you've broken it, you poor darling,' said Dad. 'Don't worry, you can go to hospital and they'll be able to plaster it up for you.'

251

'Will you take me to the hospital, Dad?'

Dad hesitated.

'*I'll* take you, Em,' said Gran, trying to push Dad out the way.

'I want my dad!' I cried.

'He's *my* dad,' said Vita.

'My dad, my dad,' said Maxie.

Dad suddenly had tears in his eyes. 'Yes, you're all my lovely kids, and of course I'm taking you to the hospital, Princess Emerald. I'll make all the doctors and nurses take excellent care of you, and we'll demand an emerald-green plaster cast for your sore arm, OK?'

'Can I have a plaster too, Dad?' Maxie begged. '*I* want a broken arm!'

'This is all your fault, Frankie, she was running after you,' said Gran.

'I know,' said Dad, a tear rolling down his cheek.

'Don't cry, Dad! It's not anyone's fault. I just fell over. I'm a big fat lump.'

'You're not at all, my baby. You've changed so much. It's so awful, I hardly recognized you!'

Dad held me tightly, and Vita and Maxie. He clung to us as if he could never bear to let us go.

'It's no use just sitting there with everyone staring! Stop play-acting with the kids and get on your mobile for an ambulance, Frankie,' said Gran. 'We've got to get Em to hospital.'

We didn't go in an ambulance. Jenna Williams's driver Bob had seen me falling. He came hurrying over to us.

'My car's just round the back of the shop in the loading bay. I'll get you to hospital in five minutes. It'll be quicker than waiting for an ambulance to get here. You're being such a brave girl,' he said to me, hauling my book bag on his back. Dad and Gran helped me up and we went round the back of the shop to the loading bay. We couldn't believe it when we saw the big shiny silver car.

'It's a Mercedes!' Gran hissed.

'I feel like a real princess!' said Vita, bouncing on the leather upholstery.

'I'm going to sit on Dad's lap in the posh car,' said Maxie.

Dad sat in the back with us, one arm round Vita, one arm round me, with Maxie on his knee. Gran sat in the front next to Bob.

'This is very kind of you,' Gran said. 'I'm so sorry to put you to all this trouble. Em, you're not bleeding, are you? Mind the upholstery!'

The hospital wasn't very far away. I wouldn't have minded if Bob had driven us to a hospital in Timbuktu. I just wanted to stay cuddled up to Dad for ever and ever and ever.

I was very scared that Dad might go as soon as we went into the Accident and Emergency area. Gran kept *telling* him to go.

'I'm staying,' Dad said firmly.

'Let me phone Julie on your mobile. Em needs her mum, not you,' said Gran.

Dad handed it over and Gran started phoning. The second she told Mum, she said she was on her way. I was so relieved, but I still had to hang onto Dad.

'I need Mum *and* Dad,' I said.

'So do I!' said Vita.

'So do I!' said Maxie.

I twisted my emerald on my poor throbbing hand and wished again.

Dad saw what I was doing. 'Still wearing your

ring, Princess Emerald?'

'Of course, Dad.'

'You'd better take it off right this minute!' said Gran.

'No!'

'You've got to. Your whole arm is starting to swell. You need to take the ring off or it'll get stuck on your finger for ever.'

'I want it to be stuck! No, Gran, please, don't take it off! *Ouch!*' I tried to jerk my hand away from her and jarred my broken arm unbearably.

'Hey, hey, leave her. Calm down, Em. Your gran's right. Come here, darling, I'll ease your ring off. Don't worry, you'll be able to wear it every day for the rest of your life, just as soon as your poor arm gets better.' Dad tenderly wriggled the ring around until he'd slipped it right off my finger. 'Have you got a pocket?'

'Can't you keep it for me in *your* pocket, Dad?'

'OK, I'll keep it safe for you, sweetheart. And I'll take Dancer to the reindeer hospital, Vita, and get her poor bent antlers fixed, and make sure she has a discreet little nose-job.' Dad looked at Maxie. 'How are your felt tips, little guy?'

Maxie wouldn't answer, just burrowing his head hard against Dad as if he wanted to bore right into him.

'They're all used up because he wrote you so many letters,' I said.

I thought Dad would be pleased but he looked as if he might start crying again.

'Yes, well might you weep,' said Gran bitterly.

The nurse came up to us and said they were ready for me to go and have an X-ray.

Gran got up and started trying to pull Vita and

254

Maxie off Dad. 'Come along, you two, we have to go with your sister,' she said briskly.

'No, I'm afraid they're not allowed. Just Emily— and maybe Daddy can come too?' the nurse suggested.

'Oh, yes please!'

So I got to go off with Dad. We stayed together while I had my arm X-rayed and then I was taken to a little room where we waited, just Dad and me.

'Are you too grown up a girl to sit on my lap?' said Dad.

'I'm not a bit too grown up,' I said, climbing on his knees. 'Just make sure I don't squash you.'

'There's nothing of you now, I'm telling you. Where's my little chubby-cheeks gone?' Dad gently poked my cheeks with his thumb and forefinger. 'Ah, at least you've still got your dimples!' he said.

'You've got thinner too, Dad,' I said.

'Ah. Well. It's because I've been missing you,' said Dad.

I reached round to the back of his neck with my good arm. I tentatively ruffled the back of his shorn spiky hair.

'When did you have your plait cut off, Dad?'

'The other month. Hannah kept nagging me, saying it was sad and pathetic, an old guy like me hanging onto his hair like a hippy, so I cut it off to shut her up.'

'Hannah?' I said, puzzled.

'My girlfriend.'

'She's called Sarah!'

'Oh. No, Sarah and I split up soon after I went up to Scotland. So then I came back down south and eventually fetched up with Hannah.'

I thought it all through in my head.

255

'What is it, Em?' said Dad.

'So you could have come to visit us all this time?' I said.

'I wanted to, darling, I wanted to so much. You've no idea just how I've missed you and Vita and Maxie—and your mum too.'

'So why didn't you?'

'I knew I wasn't wanted. It was going to be a clean break, remember? That's what your mum wanted.'

'She just said that because she was cross with you then. She didn't really *mean* it.'

'You were all pretty cross with me. I felt dreadful. I thought maybe you were better off without me. I didn't want you all getting so upset and angry. I honestly thought it was for the best.'

I looked at Dad.

'Don't look at me like that, Em, I can't bear it,' said Dad. 'All right, all right, I didn't *really* think that. I just couldn't stand all the rows and the sadness and feeling that it was all my fault. I always want everyone to be happy. Then *I'm* happy too. So I tried to put you all out of my mind, and I know I should have kept in touch, I should have sent your mum money, though I truly didn't make much. That's another reason why I went—I've been such a failure, I can't make a go of anything, I just don't seem to get the breaks. So I thought a fresh start, a new love, it would all work out for me. Only it didn't.'

'It would never work with that Sarah, she was horrible,' I said.

'Well. I'm no catch,' said Dad.

'What about Hannah?'

'I don't know. It's early days.'

'Dad. Come back to us.'

'I *want* to, Em. But it's not that simple. There's your gran for a start. We all know she can't stand me.'

'Gran's got this boyfriend though. He lives in Spain, she's talking about living over there with him. She's even spending this Christmas with him—she won't always be around.'

'Ye gods, your gran's got a *boyfriend*?' said Dad. 'I don't believe it!'

'His name's Eddie. We all thought he was after Mum at first, but it was Gran he fancied.'

'He must be mad!' Dad paused. 'What about your mum? Has she got her own boyfriend now?'

'Oh, Dad. Mum doesn't want any boyfriends. She wants you.'

'I've been such an idiot, haven't I, Princess Emerald? How are we going to make everything end happily ever after, eh? How are we going to reunite foolish King Francesco with poor long-suffering Queen Juliana?'

He started spinning me this long fairy tale. My arm was starting to throb so painfully it was hard to concentrate. The rest of me was hurting too, my arms, my neck, my head. It was as if I'd been shaken up all over.

I tried so hard to believe what Dad was saying, but I didn't know if he meant it or whether he was just making up a fairy story. I didn't know what was real any more. When I closed my eyes all my dreams had come true and Dad had his arms round me, telling me a wonderful story and making everything better. But when I looked at him properly he seemed so different, not really like *Dad*. He was just this pale thin man with short

257

spiky hair and a grubby denim jacket, telling me a whole lot of stories.

It was easier keeping my eyes closed. I was so worn out with all the amazing things that had happened I could feel my head nodding.

'That's it, sweetheart, have a little sleep,' Dad said softly.

I think I must have napped for a while, because I was dreaming I was running after Dad all over again, and then when I hurled myself at him he stepped sideways and I found myself tumbling down a hole in the pavement, down down down in pitch blackness, and I started screaming.

'Em, darling! It's all right, I'm here. Does your arm hurt really badly?' said Dad. 'The nurse has just come, pet, they're ready to plaster you up.'

I clung to Dad, scared that it might be very painful. It *did* hurt when they gently but firmly straightened my arm out.

'There we go. We'll have you right as rain in no time,' said the young doctor, smiling at me. 'There's no complications. It's a nice clean break.'

I winced at those two words.

'Sorry, pet, it'll all be over soon,' said the doctor, misunderstanding. 'Now, you have a very important decision to make. What colour plaster would you like? We can do you a very pretty pink, a fetching shade of blue—or what about a vivid emerald-green?'

'I told you so, Em,' said Dad triumphantly. 'There. You can truly be Princess Emerald now.'

I laughed uneasily, suddenly a little embarrassed for Dad to be talking about the whole princess thing in front of the doctor.

Dad went on and on about Princess Emerald as

they wound a bandage tightly round my arm and sloshed on the plaster. I knew he was only doing it to distract me. He was being so sweet. But somehow it wasn't working.

'Em's been my Princess Emerald ever since she was little,' Dad told the nurse. 'Look, she's all dressed up in green today. She's even got wondrous emerald hair!'

'That's because I was going to see Jenna Williams, Dad, and she's got this book *The Emerald Sisters*, see?'

Dad saw. He nodded a little sadly. 'Oh well. I guess you're getting too old for my fairy stories,' he said.

'No, Dad! I didn't mean it like that. I'm sorry!' I said quickly.

'It's OK, sweetheart. You're not the one who should say sorry,' said Dad.

I wasn't sure what we were talking about again. It was so hard to make sense of anything when my arm hurt and I was so tired and my head felt so fuzzy. I hung onto Dad with my good hand, gripping him very tightly.

A nurse popped her head round the door. 'How are we getting on here? Oh good, nearly done. Emily, your mum's here.'

'Mum!'

Mum came rushing in, very pale, her make-up smudged, her hair tangled. She scarcely looked at Dad. She came over to me and put her head against mine.

'Oh Em, darling, are you all right?'

'I'm fine, Mum. I've just broken my arm, that's all,' I said.

'How did you *do* it?' Mum glanced at Dad, then

back to me. 'Gran said Dad knocked you *over*!'

'God, that woman!' said Dad.

'It was me, Mum, I saw Dad and I ran after him, and then I fell. It wasn't *Dad's* fault!' I said.

'How could you ever think I'd knock her over, Julie?' said Dad.

Mum shook her head. 'I didn't really believe it. I'm not even sure Mum did either. So, Frankie, what are you doing here?'

Dad smiled weirdly at Mum. 'I suppose I've come back,' he said. 'I still love you, Julie. I want to be with you and the kids. Say you'll take me back.'

'What?' said Mum, sounding dazed. 'Look, let's just concentrate on Em and her broken arm for the moment.' She shook her head apologetically at the doctor and nurse.

'Take no notice of us,' said the nurse, smiling. 'We're used to all sorts in here. It's our very own soap opera, night after night.'

She pinned a sling on my new bright-green arm with a flourish. 'There you go, little green girl. Off you go with Mum and Dad.'

We walked down the corridor together, Mum with her arm round me, Dad still holding my good hand.

'Come on, Em, let's get you home,' Mum said wearily. 'We'd better go and find poor Gran. I think Vita and Maxie are driving her round the bend.'

'Don't go back to her, not for a few minutes,' said Dad. 'Look, let's go and have a coffee somewhere and talk.'

'Frankie, Em's exhausted, we all are. We just need to get *home*,' said Mum.

'Well, I'll come too.'

Mum paused. 'You don't really mean it. You're

just feeling all shaken up because of Em.'

'Well, of course I'm shaken up, but that's a good thing, isn't it? I've missed you so, you and the kids.'

'I bet you've hardly given us a second thought,' Mum said. She didn't even sound angry, she just sounded weary.

'I think of you nearly all the time!'

'You haven't been in touch for months and months. You haven't sent a penny for the kids in ages. They could have starved for all you've cared,' said Mum.

'I know, I've got no real excuse, but I swear I've been thinking about them. That's why I was up in London today, I was going to get a signed copy of Jenna Williams's latest book for our Em and send it as a special surprise.'

'It would have been a surprise, all right,' said Mum.

'What's up with you, Julie? You seem so . . . hard.'

'I suppose I've had to toughen up a bit,' said Mum. 'Not before time. Anyway. We're going home now. If you want to stay in touch that will be wonderful, especially for the kids. But we can't just wave a magic wand and pretend all this year hasn't happened.'

'It *hasn't* happened,' Dad said urgently. 'We're rewinding right the way back to before Christmas. We're still a family, you, me and the kids, and we all love each other and it's all going to work out, you'll see. It *will* work, won't it, Em, if we wish hard enough?'

I started crying.

'Don't, Frankie. Don't do this to her. It's been hard enough on her as it is,' said Mum. 'Come on,

Em, we're going home. You go now, Frankie, please.'

Dad insisted on ordering a taxi for all of us, saying we couldn't possibly make our way home on the train. We all squashed in together, Dad too.

'He's not coming back to *my* house,' said Gran. 'God, what do you look like, Frankie? Are you dossing down in the gutter nowadays? Have you run out of stupid girlfriends so you're trying to sponge off us again?'

'I'm just seeing my family back safe and sound, you mean-spirited old witch,' said Dad.

'Stop it, both of you,' said Mum fiercely. 'Think about the kids, please.'

Maxie and Vita sprawled on Dad's lap, half asleep. I curled up beside him, my head on his shoulder. I so badly wanted to believe in magic and wishes and fairy stories. I wanted the taxi to turn into an emerald chariot and whisk us off to an enchanted land where we could all live happily ever after. But we ended up at Gran's house instead, and the taxi fare was so much that Dad couldn't pay it, and Gran started goading him again, reaching for her purse.

'*I'm* paying this,' said Mum.

'I'll send you the cash tomorrow, Julie,' Dad said.

'Yes, you do that,' said Mum.

'You don't trust me, do you? I don't blame you. But you wait and see. Believe in me just this once,' said Dad.

He kissed Vita and Maxie and me goodbye. He kissed Mum too. She didn't put her arms round him. She just walked away, but when we were back in the house I saw she was crying.

262

I couldn't sleep much at all that night. I couldn't turn over and snuggle down because of my arm. I lay flat on my back, stiff and sore, staring into the darkness. I didn't know whether I could believe in my dad or not.

I didn't know whether he wanted to stay with his new girlfriend to come and live with us.

I didn't know whether he really had been going to get me a Jenna Williams book.

I didn't know whether he thought my ring was a real emerald.

I didn't know whether I'd ever get it back again anyway.

I didn't know whether my wish had come true or not.

Fourteen

We stayed up very very late on Christmas Eve. We huddled on the sofa, Mum, Vita, Maxie and me, eating our way through the huge tin of Christmas Quality Street. I knew Mum had bought me a pair of seriously cool kids' designer jeans for my Christmas present. They were a large size, but I was still thrilled to be able to squeeze into them. It was going to be more of a squeeze tomorrow, after all the chocolate, but I didn't care. I kept shoving one sweet after another into my mouth, even though I didn't really like chocolate so much nowadays.

Vita and Maxie were half asleep, cuddled up like puppies, chocolate drool round their mouths. I'd made us all little wine glasses out of the coloured cellophane on the sweets, and they wore theirs on their fingers.

Mum had a real wine glass in her hand, and had got through most of a bottle by herself. 'Don't you tell your gran!' she said, as I poured her the last little slurp.

'She's probably swigging back the vino too with

old Eddie,' I said. 'I don't want to be mean but it's soooo much nicer having Christmas without her.'

'Yes, it's great, just the four of us,' Mum said, though her voice wobbled a little. Maybe it was the wine.

'Not four. Five!' said Maxie. He flipped his fingers, counting. 'One, two, three, four, five.'

'Shut up, Maxie,' I said quickly. I couldn't bear him to keep on hoping.

'Four of us . . . and Father Christmas,' Mum said. 'So you kids had better go to bed in case he doesn't come in the night.'

Vita sat up, stretching. 'Is there really a Father Christmas?' she said.

'Of course there is. Who do you think leaves your presents at the end of the bed?' said Mum.

Vita's little face screwed up. 'I know who leaves the presents,' she said. 'I know who gave me Dancer.'

I put my finger to my lips and nodded at Maxie. Mum and I held our breath. Vita thought it over, and then decided she liked being one of the big girls with us. She put her own finger to her lips. She cuddled Dancer, rubbing her nose against her soft velvet.

Dancer had been posted back in a pink-tissue lined jiffy bag, as good as new, her antlers straightened, a perfect pink nose at the tip of her snout. She was wearing new pink striped pyjamas and a rose fluffy towelling dressing gown with a tiny handkerchief in the pocket. She had a little suitcase carefully packed with a party frock and a pinafore and her special pink ballet dress.

Maxie had a padded parcel too, with a brand-new set of felt pens, and a special pack of letters

268

and envelopes and a booklet of first-class stamps.

I had a little parcel, specially registered. My emerald ring had been sent back to me in a jewellery box studded with green sparkly jewels. When I opened the lid a little ballet dancer twirled round while music played.

Dad had sent Mum a red beaded purse in the shape of a heart, stuffed full of money.

He hadn't come to see us—but he hadn't forgotten us.

It was silly to hope for anything more. These were our Christmas presents this year.

We still hoped, all the same.

We sat up until we heard midnight striking.

'Happy Christmas, darlings,' Mum said, kissing us. 'Come on, into bed, all of you. Help me, Em, I'm all woozy. Oh dear, I'm a terrible mum.'

'No you're not, you're the best mum in the whole world,' I said, giving her a hug.

I picked Maxie up and herded Vita in front of me. We all three tumbled into bed, and Mum lay down on the covers beside us, kissing us all goodnight.

'Are the socks still empty?' Maxie mumbled.

'So far,' said Mum sleepily. 'Oh, dear Lord, Mother Christmas is going to have to get busy.'

'*Father* Christmas, silly,' said Maxie.

'Whatever,' said Mum. 'Night-night then, sweethearts. Sleep tight.'

She stood up and staggered a little.

'Are you OK, Mum? Hey, I'll put you to bed, shall I?' I said, sitting up.

'No, no, I'm fine. I'm just so stupid. I'm like you, Em, wishing and wishing. How stupid is that?'

'Wishes never come true the way you want,'

I said.

Then we heard a noise downstairs. A tapping at the door. Then the letter box banging.

'Who's that?' Mum called, her voice high-pitched.

'Ho ho ho!' someone called.

We all four sat up, and then we jumped up and started running downstairs. It looked like there was a Father Christmas after all. Maybe it was going to be the best Christmas ever.